AF491167

ALSO BY BEN FARTHING

Series: *I Found Horror*

I Found a Circus Tent In the Woods Behind My House

I Found Puppets Living In My Apartment Walls

I Found Christmas Lights Slithering Up My Street

Trilogy: *Horror Lurks Beneath*

It Waits On the Top Floor

They Cling To the Hull

We Hide Our Faces

Standalone Books

The Piper's Graveyard

Those Who Dwell Below the Sidewalk

Crowded Chasms: Tales In Terrifying Places

I FOUND A LOST HALLWAY IN A DYING MALL

I FOUND HORROR

BEN FARTHING

1

___

I saw a mannequin's head dragging itself across the dusty floor of a shuttered Sharper Image.

It was March sixteenth, a week after Hank told me he wanted us to move up to Fairfax with our daughter and grandson.

I'd told my manager, Helen, that I was taking my thirty. She always humphed when I told her instead of asking permission, but she couldn't fire me. Who else would take a job at Dillard's department store, when corporate announced another store closure every month? And it's not like any of the young girls could be trusted to accurately count a cash drawer.

So I left my assistant manager name tag beneath the perfume counter, set down my sample of *Eau du Pontificate*, and walked out of the empty Dillard's into the very empty Cloverleaf Mall, where Hank waited for me. He still wore his blue apron, since untying the knot in the back was difficult ever since his stroke. He offered me a bite of his daily free Auntie Anne's pretzel. I declined, since he had a habit of not eating enough, but he could easily wolf down an entire pretzel by himself.

We started our daily walk which led past a hundred empty storefronts and the not-dead-yet food court, to the Macy's that was still clinging to life across the mall.

In my twenty years working here, I'd watched each of these stores close, until all that remained were the food court, two anchor stores, and a handful of shops that clung to each of those points of life like vultures desperate for scraps.

A T-Mobile reseller had the shop next to Dillard's, across from a Christian bookstore. I waved to a familiar clerk on our way past.

Hank and I walked without speaking, since our current disagreement had no resolution yet.

The mall had finally switched the Christmas music over to love songs back in February, but now a month later it was still playing the same thirty tracks of instrumental yacht rock.

Fake ferns and empty kiosks sat in the center of the hallway, atop the white and pastel green tile. A similar color scheme was painted in stripes along the walls above the stores.

Hank broke the silence. "Please let's tell her yes."

Our daughter, Marissa, had been offered the first big job of her career. But it was up in Fairfax, right outside

D.C., a two-hour drive up 95 when there was no traffic, and there was always traffic. She'd invited us to share an apartment. Hank could quit his job at Aunt Annie's—which was always beneath his computer certificates anyways—and I could try to find another retail assistant manager position.

I told Hank what I'd been saying for the past month. "Let's not decide that yet."

He grumbled. Whether he couldn't find a more articulate response because the stroke had scrambled his speech center or because he was angry, I couldn't say. At least, I didn't want to.

But today, I didn't care for walking without chatting. For some reason, Marissa's invitation had me remembering what this empty mall used to be. Thousands of daily visitors exploring over two hundred shops. When I'd been a junior clerk at Dillard's, I'd felt like I was an integral part of this living, breathing place. And you know what? I still did.

The customers had trickled away, followed by the most of the stores, but I was still keeping this place alive. Every time I helped a soon-to-be mother-in-law pick out a dress to stand out at her son's wedding, or every time I helped a back-to-schooler choose this year's wardrobe, or every time I sold a customer on a store credit card, I was pumping a bit of lifeblood into what Cloverleaf Mall used to be and what it still was.

"I want to keep seeing Marissa and Jake every day," Hank said carefully.

I sighed. This decision wasn't only about our feelings.

"My health insurance covers your medicine. If I switch jobs, we'll only be able to afford the generic. You scared me the last time you tried the cheap stuff. I don't want to worry about you like that again."

Hank offered a loving laugh. "I'll be fine."

"Probably," I granted him. "But maybe not."

My flats clicked on the tile floor.

It felt like the noise called attention to me, but from whom, I couldn't say. Since the Christmas rush, we'd rarely passed a single soul on our walks.

The tapping was not keeping time with my steps.

I stopped walking.

A moment later, so did Hank. "What is it?"

The tapping noise continued. Every handful of *taps,* a scraping noise interrupted.

"Do you hear that?" I asked.

He tilted his head like our old cocker spaniel and then nodded.

We looked around.

Taptaptaptaptap scraaaape.

Hank leaned on a dusty bench which faced an empty kiosk designed to look like a merchant's cart.

Gray metal gates were pulled down over all the stores. Inside each one, the lights were out.

We'd stopped in front of the old Sharper Image. I used to love going in there and laughing at the high prices they demanded for such useless junk. It'd been so bright and slick in there. Now, matted dust covered the floor and the bare, shadowy shelves.

I pointed through the closed garage-door-style gate, with its grid of pinky-width metal bars. "It's coming from in there."

Something glistened on the floor. A mannequin head lay on its cheek, facing away from us.

A plastic arm attached seamlessly to the thing's neck. Its plastic skin reflected the fluorescent lights of the main corridor, a shiny surface contrasting with dingy surroundings.

The mannequin head faced the Sharper Image's back wall, for which I felt a deep gratitude. It wanted to look at me, to satiate some dark curiosity, and if it did I wouldn't like the result. Yet with nightmare logic I expected it to roll over and open its plastic eyelids.

I stayed perfectly still, suddenly too scared to even reach out for my husband.

The absurdity of the situation overcame my silly fear. I was being immature, not the calm and collected person my family relied upon.

I tried to sound casual. "What's that, do you think?"

As we watched, the mannequin fingers stretched forward to tap one at a time on the tile floor. Then they flexed to drag the head and arm forward a few inches.

Taptaptaptaptap, scraaaaape.

Hank laughed, albeit nervously. "It's a leftover from that Halloween store."

Maybe. Except, I'd poked around in there, imagining costumes for our grandson until I saw the prices. There'd been evil clown masks and plenty of zombie makeup, but no mannequin heads with arms grafted to their necks. Plus, the Spirit Halloween had been in the opposite end of the mall.

Spencer's Gifts used to live a few shops down. This could be some novelty left behind.

It calmed my nerves, having a puzzle to solve. I don't know why the thing spooked me so bad at first.

"But who turned it on?" I wondered aloud.

The mannequin fingers froze mid-stretch, as if reacting to my voice.

My breath caught in my throat.

Slowly, the head turned. The indent of its left eye came into view, then its nose, then the indent of its right eye.

I couldn't look away, waiting for those plastic eyelids to peel back and reveal the organic machinery making this thing tick.

Hank exhaled sharply. "Oof. Made me jump." He stuttered out a chuckle.

His laugh was a wave of reassurance.

Of course the mannequin head didn't open its eyes. I don't know why I expected it to.

But it still felt like it was looking at me. The sunken places on either side of its nose drilled into me with curiosity—yes, I was sure it was *curiosity* because I felt it with some preternatural empathy.

Again, I was being silly.

I reached for Hank's arm, to keep him physically steady and myself internally so. "It's creepy."

"Yup," he agreed. "Let's keep walking."

Hank pulled me along with steps that were still a bit jilting. I wanted to look back at the mannequin head's eye sockets, test whether I felt its curiosity about me again, but I was Hank and Marissa's anchor and I couldn't entertain silly fears.

2

———

IT TURNS out I could very much entertain silly fears. I couldn't get that mannequin head out of my mind, or the sense that it had been *curious* about me.

When we reached the food court, I told Hank I didn't remember if I'd locked my drawer and I needed to cut our walk short.

I headed back toward the Sharper Image, alone.

My heart pounded with fear, but I wanted answers about what we'd just seen. I'd kept my family safe for twenty-nine years, and that didn't happen by accident. It happened by being prepared.

I was not prepared for what happened next.

Cloverleaf's main artery—running from Dillard's, past the food court, all the way to Macy's—is not the only hallway in the mall. There are branching paths.

As I passed one such path, someone shouted from

down among the closed shops. It was an angry, confused noise that drifted from around a corner.

I would have ignored it.

Down there was what we called the Sears wing. Sears was the first big anchor store to close. If you walked down this side hallway, and turned to your left as you reached the papered-over glass doors of the JCPenney, then you'd see a long straightaway guiding you to the old Sears. Something like fifteen shops long. There used to be an affordable women's boutique down that way that I frequented on my breaks.

But when Sears closed, the foot traffic dried up and all the little shops down this way couldn't stay afloat.

I often wondered why the mall owner didn't block off the whole hallway. More than once, I'd seen security escorting away a homeless person who'd tried to escape the cold by camping out in the abandoned Sears wing.

And so I would have ignored the angry, confused shout that I heard coming from past the JCPenney, around the corner.

Except.

It wasn't a wordless shout.

The voice—male, elderly—had shouted, "Close the knife before you pocket it."

At least, I thought that's what it was.

And here's the thing: my old coworker Saswin used to sing those words as he opened boxes of perfume.

Saswin retired—or quit, I suppose, since he was only part-time and thus received no retirement—when his early-onset-dementia ending up onsetting even earlier than the doctors anticipated. In those last months that we worked together, he'd hum that little ditty on repeat.

It had been eight years since I'd heard Saswin's catchy safety song.

But I heard the melody now, partly masked by the tone of the confused shout, but still there. It rose in pitch through "close the knife" and then dropped for "pocket it," like I remembered Marissa humming at four-years-old pretending to be a superhero. *Bum dadadaaaaaa!*

The shout came again, more of a groan this time. It sounded farther away.

I didn't want to go down that way, or even poke my head around the corner. The whole Sears wing felt like the walkway between pews in an old church, leading up to the pulpit where the pastor used to preach before everyone fell away from the gospel.

I'd just as soon enjoy my job without seeing a visual argument that Cloverleaf wasn't what it used to be.

And so I hesitated, even when I knew it was Saswin.

His call echoed again, garbled but still sounding like, "Close the knife before you pocket it!"

Worry filled me up, pushing aside my feelings about the Sears wing.

Dementia patients wandered, didn't they? Had Saswin woken up this morning, eight years after retirement, convinced that he was late for work? He'd have rushed over—Saswin had been punctual to a fault.

But Cloverleaf had changed in eight years. Saswin

wouldn't recognize the mall. When he'd left, it'd been filled with families and girls-nights-out and teenagers dropped off on their own too young. Every storefront in the mall had been home to a unique shop.

If that's the mall Saswin remembered, then how would he feel to wander in here now and see the lines of gated, empty shops, shelves bare and tile floors in need of a good sweep?

He'd feel like the world had left him behind.

I checked my watch. Since I'd cut my walk short, I had a whole ten minutes until Helen needed me back.

And if that was Saswin I was hearing, I couldn't leave him feeling confused and abandoned.

I walked down the branching hallway, toward the locked and papered glass doors of the old JCPenney.

The garbled shout came again, still with that melody, but this time I couldn't convince myself the words were the same. It didn't sound like, "Close the knife before you pocket it," but rather something else.

Was this my old coworker at all? Or some poor homeless person who the world had forgotten? I supposed whoever it was might need help. If it was nobody I knew, then I'd keep my distance and call security. I'd rather leave the whole thing alone, but I was the sort of person who stepped up and helped out. Despite what others might think, I wasn't fading with age. I was still *me*.

"Saswin?" I came around the corner at a distance, in case someone was waiting just out of sight.

No one was. I saw the chapel-like walkway, but now it

felt more like a gauntlet: two rows of failed shops encroached on the path to their dead mother—that mammoth-sized corporate failure straight ahead.

It was farther to the Sears than I remembered.

My strange feelings toward this wing of the mall didn't matter, because it turned out that I should have trusted my ears:

His back to me, talking to someone out of sight, stood my old friend Saswin.

3

___

Saswin repeated himself as I hurried over. He still spoke to whoever was there with him.

"Close the knife before you pocket it!"

He and his companion—who he blocked from my view with his body—were nearly all the way to the Sears.

I passed the closed Bath & Body Works, its pungent mishmash of odors still emanating from the empty shelves behind the gate.

It shared a wall with a dead Gamestop, which was still called Babbages when I'd bought Marissa her first Gameboy Color.

Happy nostalgia tried to drift into my mind, but my worry for my old coworker maintained control. Maybe Saswin's companion had a handle on things, but I had to check. I couldn't let Saswin think he'd been left behind.

As I approached, the person he was talking to came into view.

Or I should say: the mannequin.

Saswin wore gray sweatpants and a black Richmond Flying Squirrels T-shirt. His dark curly hair had gained some white since I'd seen him last, and his cheeks were lined with wrinkles, visible even under his weeklong beard stubble. We'd had a 60th birthday party for him and commented about how he looked so young. That couldn't last forever, I supposed.

Saswin was a short man, and so he had to tilt his head backward to look the mannequin in the eyes.

Or not "eyes," but those blank plastic recesses above the blank plastic nose and below the blank plastic scalp.

The whole mannequin was naked, whatever clothing it once advertised now long gone.

The sight of the mannequin discomforted me, after what Hank and I had seen that morning. That had been a remote-controlled freakshow contestant—I was glad to see that this mannequin was more than a head and arm.

But it was still just a mannequin, which meant it fell on me to make sure that Saswin's daughter knew where he was.

I reached out to touch his shoulder but then thought better of it.

I backed up so I could speak his name without spooking him. "Saswin," I said gently. "I'm Lisa. We worked together at Dillard's." I purposely slurred the "-ed" of "worked" as to let him continue believing that it was still eight years ago, if that's where his mind was right now. "I heard you singing your rhyme about your utility knife."

I waited for him to respond.

The architecture of the Sears wing kept away the noise from the food court. Even the ceiling speakers that played music in the rest of the mall weren't switched on here, although I could just barely make out the instrumental love ballads drifting up from Cloverleaf's main drag, around the corner in front of the JCPenny.

He suddenly jerked in surprise, gasped, whipped around. He saw me and the fear in his wide eyes melted into mirth. "You got here quick!"

"You remember me?" Oh good. This would be easier than I'd worried.

But instead of answering my question, Saswin waved for me to follow him. "There's ninety minutes before the evening rush gets in. That leaves us time to crush a few Tommy Girl samples."

He offered me his elbow like he was a courtier at a ball. I gave him my hand. "Why don't we sit down and I can call someone for you? Where are you living now? Still with your daughter?"

"My daughter," Saswin said, but not in a tone that answered my question. "I retired."

His cheeks turned dark in embarrassment. He was having a flash of coherency, an inverse of the flashes that hit Hank these days.

"Let's walk back to Dillard's and you can say hi to Helen. We'll call your daughter." I tugged at his elbow but he didn't budge. "Do you know your daughter's phone number?"

I didn't have it saved, but I might have Saswin's old cell number. With my free hand, I scrolled through my contacts. There it was. I called, but it was disconnected.

Saswin suddenly shoved the mannequin. It clattered to the tile floor. "Where are the shoppers? It's Saturday."

It was Tuesday, but I wasn't going to argue about that.

"Come on," I tugged with more force. "Let's head this way."

Saswin refused to budge. "I can't fall behind on my metrics."

God, Helen was the worst when it came to reportable numbers. She'd imprinted the fear so deep in Saswin that it was still hanging around.

I needed to call somebody.

This felt like the purpose for the police non-emergency line, but I didn't know that number, so I used my cell to call 911.

A young man's voice answered. "Nine-one-one, what's the nature of your emergency?"

"I'm sorry," I said. "I don't know the other numbers to call, but I've found an old coworker with dementia. I think he wandered back to where he used to work."

"What's the address of where you're located?"

"Cloverleaf Mall." I gave him the street address, which I'd memorized long ago while filling out bank deposits. "That's for the Dillard's, though. We're in the old Sears wing."

"I need the address, ma'am. Does the Sears wing have

an address?" He sounded too young to remember the Sears. Although as he kept talking, he actually sounded much older. As old as Saswin and me.

"I don't know, but if you tell them to drive a circle around the mall, they'll see it."

"Ma'am?" The operator's voice was definitely elderly. How had I ever thought he was young? "Do you have an address?"

"I don't—"

Saswin's voice came through the phone, even as I stood next to him with my hand hooked in his elbow. "Where is everybody, ma'am?"

My old coworker kicked the downed mannequin. His lips didn't part and yet his voice came through the phone. "They've left me behind. You won't leave me, too, will you?"

"No," I whispered. "Of course not."

What was happening?

Had someone slipped me drugs? Was there mold in the air?

Saswin—the physical Saswin, here in front of me—shook free from my hand. He walked around a fern and headed toward the old Sears. He opened one of the papered-over glass doors.

"Wait," I said.

He looked back at me. Through the door, I saw a row of eight escalators positioned shoulder-to-shoulder. All of them going up.

Saswin's answer came from both his mouth and the voice on the phone. "You won't leave me behind." Not a question or an order but a self-comforting mantra.

He entered the Sears.

As the door wheezed shut between us, the 911 call went dead.

4

———

MY FIRST INSTINCT was to follow Saswin. Don't let him out of my sight. He must be so scared, lost in the empty mall he remembered from the prime of its life.

So even as I struggled to explain the 911 call, or why I'd seen eight escalators going up inside Sears, I still had to follow my old friend. Bring him back to where he felt safe.

I made it three steps before I heard plastic clattering behind me. I turned back around fast enough that my hip protested with a little surge of pain.

The mannequin was on its feet, not three feet away from me.

Impossible.

I'd watched Saswin shove it down. I'd heard it hit the tile floor.

Now it stood facing sideways, giving me a view of its profile.

A plastic arm stuck out from the mannequin's lower

back. The extra elbow came to an unnaturally narrow point. The fingers, each with an extra knuckle, rested on the nape of the mannequin's neck.

The strangeness of it paralyzed me. I stared not at the deformities of the arm itself but at the point where it met the rest of the mannequin. The white, shiny plastic had the slight bulge of a male shoulder. It blended seamlessly with the thing's plastic back.

Just like the head-and-arm combo Hank and I had seen earlier, this could be the Picasso art project of some weirdo—but it should have been more obvious where the grafted arm met the original figure. Even if it was melted together, there'd be bumps where heated plastic had bonded to itself.

But the arm connected to the thing's back like it had all been made as one single piece.

Where the head-and-arm thing in the Sharper Image had been a creepy oddity, this larger mannequin gave off a more threatening aura. In the animal kingdom, size meant strength. I wondered if the same was true of mannequins.

I looked at the doors to Sears, wondering if Saswin had been afraid of the strange mannequin, too. Maybe that's why he'd shoved the thing.

Movement in the corner of my eye. I turned back to my plastic companion.

Unmoving as a stone, the mannequin's extra arm now reached for me, extra-jointed fingers splayed just inches in front of my face.

I tried to gasp. My lungs caught and for a second I thought I was having a heart attack.

Then precious oxygen found its way inside. I sucked it in greedily and backed away until I bumped into the closed gate of a Sam Goody music store.

With the whole gauntlet of closed shops around me, all I could see was the three-armed mannequin.

It had moved.

Somehow, when I was looking away, the mannequin had reached for me.

I didn't dare take my eyes off it again.

My mind flashed to ghosts and demons and sci-fi TV shows.

I wanted to flee wildly but my legs couldn't take me as fast as they once could.

And I couldn't give in to silly fears. That's not who I was.

I breathed deep. This wasn't as bizarre as it seemed.

The damned thing was like the head and arm that Hank and I had seen earlier. Must be motors inside.

It had reacted to me—moved when I looked away—which meant someone was watching and operating it via remote control.

I squeezed my eyes shut. Counted to three. Opened them.

The mannequin had closed half the distance between us. It had turned around so that awful extra arm was out of sight.

The operator had to be hiding somewhere in front of me, because they'd seen me close my eyes.

I looked for someone hiding behind the fake ferns up ahead, or peeking out from behind the metal slats of a shop's gate.

Nobody popped out from hiding, but the mall had security cameras. This could be a bored security guard playing tricks.

Except, how did Saswin play into it?

Because I didn't believe in coincidences.

My heart still pounded. The hairs on my arms stood on end.

I was trying so hard to logically explain this mannequin but my gut wasn't convinced.

I turned, eyes still on the mannequin, and took a backward step toward the JCPenney. I bumped into something light and wobbly.

It rocked away and then bumped lightly back into me.

It made a hollow plastic sound as it scraped on the tile floor.

I didn't want to take my eyes off the mannequin in front of me, but I'd quickly become familiar with the sound of plastic feet scraping on tile. I knew what I'd heard.

I slowly stepped to the side, keeping my eyes on the first mannequin. I gave a quick glance to what I'd collided with:

Another mannequin.

It stood in arm's reach, another approximation of a

person in smooth plastic. It was missing its right arm. Instead, a second head protruded sideways out from its shoulder.

From its two heads, four blank ivory recesses regarded me coldly.

In a panic, I shoved the mannequin hard in the chest. My palm slapped against the plastic. It toppled backward to clatter on the floor. The sound echoed in both directions up the empty mall, with longer intervals between each echo than I expected.

I looked around.

The Sears wing felt bigger, the exit farther away.

Before I could gather my senses, something reached for my elbow. I turned to see the first mannequin, closer but motionless, now stretching its neck in a position of lunging for me. Its unnatural appendage had reached around from behind its back to try to clamp those elongated fingers onto my arm.

It had frozen when I'd turned to look at it.

Not just stopped moving, with a slide to a halt and a slight rocking from the sudden stop in momentum, but totally frozen, as if it had never moved at all.

My mouth went dry.

These things had to be remote-controlled machines, but the more they stalked me, the less I could believe that.

Air wouldn't enter my lungs. I needed to flee, needed to get outside and breathe the crisp winter air.

I heard plastic scraping on the floor. I backed away, trying to get both mannequins in my sight.

The second mannequin froze in place in the act of getting to its feet.

I couldn't believe any of this. I had a husband, daughter, and grandson at home who relied on me. I didn't have the luxury of entertaining nonsense fears.

But the harder I tried not to believe what I was seeing, the more firmly panic cranked up the pressure in my head and lungs.

I gasped but couldn't get my fill. I tried again. The need for air overpowered both my confusion and my need to get away.

The mall blurred, shops and kiosks and benches receding even farther.

I saw the vague figure of the second mannequin get to its feet with stuttery movement. The first mannequin stepped jerkily toward me. No, away from me, in the direction that Saswin had gone.

I backed away, tripped over my feet, fell to my knees. The impact with the tile jolted every bone in my body, but nothing broke.

The pain in my knees dislodged my mind from its panic.

Sweet air rushed down my pipes.

My view of the mall came back into focus, along with the two mannequins, once again frozen.

The Sears felt farther away than it should be. The exit from this hallway past the JCPenney was farther, too.

A new fear sprouted in my mind.

If I didn't believe the mannequins were moving with

remote-controlled robotics, and I couldn't believe that they were somehow marching around of their own volition, then the problem must be inside my own mind.

The second mannequin's extra head watched me with sideways blank eyes.

The first mannequin still had its third hand outstretched.

I backed away, eyes on them both, while trying to gauge where I now stood.

Fear of senility bloomed in my addled mind. Maybe Marissa was right. We should move in with her.

If I faced the JCPenney, I'd be turning my back on the mannequins. I kept them in view while I backed directly away from the Sears. That should aim me right at the corner that would lead back to the mall's main drag.

I took it slowly because a backwards fall could shatter my hip.

With every step, my thighs ached. Walking backwards used muscles I hadn't activated in years. But the mannequins got farther away.

After a few dozen steps, I risked a glance behind me.

My destination was getting closer. This was working.

I turned my head back.

The mannequins posed in reaching positions, only ten feet away. They'd shot forward twenty feet.

No more glances behind me—I kept my eyes on the mannequins, locking them in place.

I told myself there was nothing weird about freezing

them with my gaze. In fact, I was showing the hiding operator that he couldn't fool me. I almost believed it.

I kept walking backwards.

I suddenly remembered why I'd come around this way in the first place.

Saswin needed help.

It'd be embarrassing to say that I'd found him wandering and then I'd ran away because two mannequins scared me. But even worse, if Saswin was hit with a moment of lucidity, he'd be in his comfortable old workplace, except it'd be empty. He'd feel totally abandoned.

I blinked. Both mannequins inched toward me.

Maybe I could circle around them, then back toward Sears.

But my gut instinct was to flee, get the heck away from these mannequins, never find out their intentions for when they reached me.

I called for Saswin once. The papered-over doors of the old Sears remained a blank barrier.

I tried not to think about the entire bank of escalators that I'd seen inside, all whirring and clicking, all going up.

There was nothing else I could do. I backed down the rest of the way out from the Sears wing, keeping the mannequins in sight. When my eyes felt dry, I blinked one at a time.

My path took me behind a stand with a map of the mall.

It broke my line of sight to the mannequins. Scuffling plastic echoed in the quiet corridor.

A mannequin head poked out from behind the map.

I wanted to look away and deny what I was seeing, but I kept my eyes glued to that plastic head.

Finally, in my periphery I saw the doors to JCPenney.

I backed around the corner to the main drag.

Music echoed loudly in the brightly lit hall. These stores were closed as well, which was sometimes eerie, but this was the path I took every day between Dillard's and the food court. I'd take the familiar eerie any day, over whatever I'd just experienced in the Sears wing.

I kept my eyes glued on the corner I'd come around, waiting for a mannequin to creep into sight.

But it seemed they intended to stay in their den.

I checked my watch.

I'd be late getting back to work, but I wanted Hank's help.

Saswin was still wandering in that Sears somewhere. I considered calling 911 again, but instead I hurried back to the food court to find my husband.

5

––––––––

I CHECKED over my shoulder a dozen times on the way to the food court, certain that the mannequins were about to catch up.

But I only saw the same empty sight as any other day: tile floors, pastel stripes on the walls, and gated shops.

In the food court, I found Hank sitting with Marissa at a table in front of Auntie Anne's.

Jake sat between them on a plastic booster seat, toddler cheeks stuffed with sweet pretzel.

The food court was decently packed—the office park across the street brought plenty of lunch traffic on week-days. Of course, at Cloverleaf, "decently packed" meant only a quarter of the tables were taken.

For a moment, I was surprised that Marissa was visiting Hank without even telling me. Was I already becoming an afterthought to her?

Then I remembered that *I* was the one who'd forgotten. Both Hank and I had, actually. Marissa had told us she'd be by, so it was convenient that I'd ended our walk early.

I approached the table, trying to breathe quietly.

Marissa immediately noticed. "Mom, are you all right?"

Hank had been busy making faces at Jake, but he picked up on Marissa's concern to inspect me with caring eyes. "What's wrong?"

"Remember my old coworker Saswin?"

Hank nodded. "Indian fellow? Dementia?"

"Pakistani. I just saw him in the old Sears wing." There were too many weird things to get across to him all at once. Before I could back up and start explaining, Marissa cut in.

"They didn't close that off?" She asked it like I was a confused old biddy.

"The space is still for lease. It's part of the mall." I huffed, which I knew Marissa hated, but it was a bad habit. "My old coworker Saswin was back there and yes, he's the one with dementia. I couldn't get him to come with me, so we need to call security or maybe the police."

I didn't say, *plus there's mannequins that tried to grab me so I don't want to go back alone.*

Hank stood up, ever the worrier. "You want to go find him?" A question, but really a statement of intent.

"No," I said too quickly. I didn't want to go back there and I definitely didn't want Hank to go off wandering around. "We have to call security first. Can I use your phone?"

"Is yours on the fritz again?" Marissa asked. "I've been telling you to upgrade."

I squeezed the phone in my hand. Saswin had spoken to me through it, even while I was looking at him right in front of me. I was afraid to press it to my ear. "The battery's dead," I lied. "It's been dying quick, lately."

"Time for a new device," Marissa was always chiming in about how I could improve my life.

Hank handed me his phone. "You call while we walk." He hated phone calls. He got embarrassed by his slow speech.

Marissa wiped cinnamon and sugar from Jake's face. "Are you guys okay if I don't come? I've got to drop Jake back off at daycare before I jump on a work call." She picked up my grandson and playfully said, "Before too long, you'll get to stay home with Grandpa while Mommy's at work."

"That's not one hundred percent decided, yet," I said.

Marissa busied herself wiping off the table. Anything to avoid eye contact now that I'd made it awkward. "I didn't mean to get ahead of you. I talked to Dad and got the impression you were in agreement about moving with us."

"It's just so crowded up there. And I'd be leaving my career."

"I understand. Do whatever's best for you guys. Jake will be just fine in a fancy daycare up in Alexandria."

Now I'd put her on the defensive. Not what I'd meant to do at all. "I'm not saying 'no.' Just that your Dad and I need to talk a bit more first." I didn't want her to move away and leave us behind, but I also didn't want to give up everything to follow her. Most of all I hated having this conversation. Couldn't she see that I could do a better job taking care of her in the home she'd grown up in? "I still think you could find a job worth taking down here somewhere."

"Mom," Marissa said, exasperated. "I've already accepted this job. The salaries up there are too good to pass up."

I locked and loaded my argument about increased cost-of-living, but Hank was well on his way out of the food court and I didn't want him to go look for Saswin by himself. "We'll talk more later," I told Marissa. I gave Jake a kiss and then hurried after Hank, dialing security as I went.

6

THE SECURITY GUARDS' office was near the food court. A young man named Jimmy was on duty. With only a dozen stores open in the mall, he approached us eagerly, looking for some action. He adjusted his belt to keep his pants up, his wrinkled blue shirt and his unshaven, greasy face giving him a disheveled appearance. "Your friend was next to the Sears?" he asked. Without slowing his gait, he gestured for me to lead the way.

Fear suddenly returned. Was I ready to face those two strange mannequins again? Or face whether my own mind had made them up?

Hank took my hand. "Okay?"

I couldn't figure out a non-crazy way to warn them, so I let the words spill out. "Mannequins chased me away before I could help Saswin."

Jimmy scoffed, which turned into a laugh and then an embarrassed cough. "Sorry. What do you mean?"

I felt my lips tighten. Jimmy wouldn't have laughed if I were younger. He had no right to write me off so quickly.

"Like the mannequin we saw this morning?" Hank spoke haltingly. My protective instinct woke up, ready to keep my husband safe during another incident of mental blankness. It distracted me from Jimmy's rudeness. But he was fine.

And of course, once Hank acknowledged we'd seen something weird this morning, Jimmy took it more seriously.

"You both saw a mannequin moving around?"

"Not a whole one," Hank said, smoothly. It must have only been a stutter. No episode for now. "A head with an arm sticking out of it. The arm moved to drag it forward. It was in the old Sharper Image, so maybe it was some robot toy left behind."

I was grateful to Hank for explaining and not leaving me high and dry to sound like a loon.

"No merchandise in there," Jimmy said. "That place has been empty for years."

"What'd you see over here?" Hank asked as we approached the JCPenney and the branching hallway to its side. "The same mannequin head as this morning?"

The three of us peered at the corner, my fear apparently contagious enough for Hank and Jimmy to join me in hesitating.

"No. These two were full bodies. Every time I looked away they got closer."

"They moved?" Jimmy's incredulity was turning into

wonder. "You think someone put mannequins on Roomba vacuums?"

"Remote controls and robotics, more likely," Hank said. "I was an electronics whiz in a past life."

Before the stroke slowed down his thoughts.

Hank stumbled over his next question. "If they only moved when you looked away, someone must have been watching you. What was Saswin doing when the mannequins moved?"

"He'd already gone inside the Sears."

"You mean he was out of sight." Jimmy clapped his hands like he'd cracked the case. "So you couldn't see him use the remote control. Let's go find him."

This was getting away from me. Saswin was wandering an empty mall, which he remembered being crowded and loud. We needed to go help him so he didn't think the world had left him behind, and here was this security guard acting like Saswin was a criminal to hunt down.

"No. Saswin wasn't controlling them. He's barely there, mentally. That's why we've got to find him and make sure he doesn't hurt himself."

"Which you didn't do before," Jimmy said, "because you got scared by remote control mannequins."

And because I'd heard Saswin's voice through the call to 911, even while I was looking right at him. But I wasn't sharing that tidbit.

"Watch your tone," Hank told Jimmy.

That powerlessness I'd felt during the phone call came

flooding back into me. I didn't want to face those mannequins again.

The younger man held up his hands in an *I surrender* gesture. "I'm only saying aloud what's happening here."

"Come on," Hank said. He led the way around the corner.

As we got close, my heart raced. What was I about to show them? I agreed with Hank, mostly—someone was controlling the mannequins via remote control. Not Saswin, but someone.

What if they'd already taken away both weird mannequins? It would look like I'd made the whole thing up.

I worried that I had. The mannequins, the 911 call, maybe even Saswin himself.

I mean, that made more sense than the alternative.

This was the last thing I needed, for Hank and Marissa to worry about my mental acuity, when I was the one who should be taking care of them. There'd be no recovering from this, either. I could already see us moving in with Marissa up in Fairfax, see her concerned, patronizing looks when I couldn't find my keys or when I forgot why I walked into a room. From here on out, every little slip would be a reminder: *Mom's not the one who cares for us anymore; now we have to take care of her.*

Hank didn't slow down for my internal worries. He walked straight ahead until he could see down the Sears wing.

He froze.

I've only ever heard Hank swear twice in my life. Once when he changing the fuel pump in our old Ford Taurus and the jack broke, dropping the car on his foot, pinning it until I could gather enough neighbors to lift it off. And then again a year ago when he was moving Marissa and newborn Jake out of our soon-to-be ex-son-in-law's apartment, and the dumb young man tried to physically block Hank from getting inside to his daughter and grandson.

But in the mall, when Hank walked around the corner and saw down the Sears wing, he whispered, "I'll be damned."

Jimmy passed the corner next. "The fuck?"

The word came more naturally to Jimmy than "damn" did to Hank.

Relief washed over me. I wasn't crazy, because Hank and Jimmy saw the two weird mannequins.

I came around the corner.

An entire crowd of mannequins filled the Sears wing.

Men, women, children, all nakedly displaying their white shiny plastic flesh, but posed as if this were a typical Saturday ten years ago.

I grabbed Hank's arm. Despite how slowly he moved these days, for thirty years he'd been my protector, and old habits die hard.

I almost asked Hank and Jimmy if they were seeing this, but that would be the perfect way to announce that I was too old to make big decisions.

The closest mannequin stood ten feet away, a woman

holding hands with a child-sized figure which leaned toward the empty shop which used to be K.B. Toys.

Jimmy exhaled, spreading the smell of a grape Black and Mild cigarillo. "You said there were two mannequins."

"There were."

Hank stuttered, couldn't get the words out, and pointed instead.

On a bench by an empty fountain sat a mannequin with a forest of plastic fingers sticking out from its head.

"What is that?" Hank managed.

After he pointed out the weirdness, I suddenly saw it everywhere in the crowd.

The little boy who wanted to go to the toy store had feet stuck out in all directions from the bottom of his legs. His mother had recesses for eyes all down her torso.

A male mannequin posed walking toward the JCPenney had his legs and arms switched.

Sitting on a bench by an empty fountain was a mannequin with plastic fingers extending out all along the length of its arms.

And standing in the crowd were two mannequins I already knew: one with an extra head instead of a right arm, and one with an arm sticking out from the small of its back.

Both were pointed so their empty eyes drilled directly into me.

"I don't know who was on the night shift," Jimmy said, "but I'm reporting him. This had to make a ton of noise. How could he have missed it?"

"It was empty twenty minutes ago," I said. I kept looking back and forth between the two mannequins from before, waiting for them to leap forward the moment my eyes were away.

An idea sent an icy flash up my spine: would *all* these mannequins move if we looked away?

I took a deep breath.

There was nothing unnatural going on. It was someone with mechanical prowess and remote controls. They couldn't control more than a couple at once.

I was spooking myself for no reason.

That's what I tried to believe, anyways.

Hank chewed on his lip. "Should we go look for Saswin?"

I didn't want to walk through a crowd of mutant-looking mannequins, putting myself where I couldn't possibly see them all at once. But my old friend needed help.

If I hadn't invented the mannequins in my head, then I hadn't dreamed up Saswin, either.

That also meant I hadn't dreamed up the 911 call. I could explain away the moving mannequins, but I had no idea how to explain Saswin talking to me through the phone when I was right there with him.

If I were a weaker person, or if I didn't have a family that relied on me to be confident and in control, then maybe I would have backed down. But that's not who I was.

"He went into the Sears," I said.

"Let's go, then." Jimmy led the way into the crowd of mannequins.

7

NOT EVERY MANNEQUIN had extra fingers, or swapped limbs, or missing facial features. And among those that did, there was a progression to the strangeness.

I spotted a perfectly average mannequin, next to another whose only defect was a missing ear. And then past that one was the mannequin with the second head sticking out of its right shoulder, still watching me.

I imagined an assembly line slowly breaking down, pumping out stranger and stranger mannequins as pulleys rotted and bearings rusted.

As Jimmy walked deeper into the plastic crowd, Hank noticed my hesitation. He took my hand and led me forward.

I couldn't protest about turning our backs on them or I'd sound like I was losing it.

I looked back over my shoulder to keep in view the mannequins we passed.

I felt Hank let go of my hand. "Weird."

"What is it?" I wanted to know what he was seeing, but I didn't dare turn back around and let the mannequins behind us out of my sight.

"This one's got a water fountain spigot stuck in its forehead."

I glanced over.

Sure enough, a polished silver water fountain nozzle was pressed sideways into the thing's plastic forehead. It looked brand new, like the mannequin had been formed with the shiny metal in the mold.

"And look at that one." Hank pointed to another mannequin back in the crowd with a green plastic fern sticking out from its belly.

Jimmy had turned around to see what was slowing us down. "Must have been factory rejects. That's how the pranksters could afford so many."

"I don't know," Hank said in the tone he used when his brain was clogged up with a thought. Or when he was responding to something he thought was stupid, but he didn't want to insult the speaker and so he pretended his own aging mind was to blame.

In this case, I agreed with Hank. The water fountain and fake fern were pieces of the mall, not of a mannequin manufacturing facility. My gut said these little bits of merging were recent.

Jimmy continued on.

I followed, again pointing my eyes behind us.

Had the mannequins moved when I wasn't looking?

Limbs posed in the act of walking but I couldn't be sure if it was different from a moment ago.

I searched the crowd until I found the mannequin with the extra arm sticking out from the small of its back. Its head was turned to look at me.

I sucked in a little gasp. I tried to hide it, but Hank surely heard me, and now he'd ask me what had frightened me.

I asked another question to quickly distract him. "Where do you think they even got all these?"

When he didn't answer right away, I risked a glance over my shoulder.

My husband was gone.

I couldn't find him in the crowd of white, shiny mannequins.

"Hank?"

Jimmy must have heard the panic in my voice. He turned around to check on us, annoyed we kept slowing him down. "What's wrong?"

I ignored him to squeeze between two mannequins, toward where I'd last seen my husband. "Where'd you go?"

Suddenly, Hank stumbled out from behind a four-armed mannequin. His eyes were wide as saucers. His cheeks were flush and sweat clung to his forehead. He saw me. Relief relaxed his whole body. "You were so far away."

I embraced him, but this was worrying. Hank hadn't had an episode like this for three months. Nannying for Jake wouldn't even be an option if these problems kept occurring. Unless I helped nanny, which meant giving up my career.

"You alright?" I asked.

His head swiveled around. He quickly stepped farther away from a mannequin. "Let's go check on Saswin."

Hank looked worried about himself, which hadn't happened in the episodes that followed his stroke. He'd always come out of them confused and angry.

But now Hank knew exactly where he was.

This wasn't a mental episode.

Something else was scaring him.

Maybe something like mannequins that move when you don't look at them.

"If you're both okay, let's keep going," Jimmy said.

I wanted to ask Hank what he'd seen, but neither of us wanted Jimmy to leave us behind in the crowd.

We followed him through to the Sears.

Jimmy rattled the closest door handle. "Locked."

"Don't you have keys?" I asked.

"Somewhere in the office." He patted a keyring on his belt. "My master key doesn't work on the big anchor stores."

Hank tried the next door. No luck. "Why didn't you bring it? We told you he went in here."

"No, you said he was in the Sears wing, not the store itself."

Hank huffed as he pulled on another stiff door handle. Six papered-over glass doors, all of them locked.

I could see the frustration in his gritted teeth. Hank

hated when feeling confused. He despised feeling scared. He always responded with anger at himself. Whatever had happened a moment ago when I couldn't find him—it had Hank rattled.

Despite the insanity around us, my mind still went to work figuring out how to cheer him up. After our shifts I could grill him some southwestern chicken. That had been his favorite meal for a year now.

But that automatic carer portion of my brain couldn't hold center stage for more than a second.

We were here to help Saswin.

I tried the door myself. Locked tight.

Paper on the opposite side of the glass flapped briefly. Not enough to reveal the inside, but I remembered the line of escalators placed next to each other, all going up to the second floor.

Jimmy had seen the paper move, too. "The central air is still going. Don't want the pipes to freeze."

"Have you been in there lately?" I asked.

"Not for a month or two. Someone else should have given it a once-over on my day off two weeks ago."

"What's inside?"

Jimmy shrugged. "Empty shelves and racks. A lot of dust."

"Is there still power to the escalators?"

"Power, yes. But they're not switched on. Why?"

Because I'd seen them. When Saswin had opened the door and gone inside, too many escalators were going up —at a quarter the normal speed, but all of them *up*.

The idea that Saswin might have wandered upstairs worried me, although I couldn't say why.

Hank checked his watch. "We don't really have time to wait for you to get the keys. Our breaks are already over."

"What about Saswin?" I asked, still dodging the real question: *What happened to you?*

Jimmy sighed. "I'll give the cops a call, since if he's in there, a wandering dementia patient is a little above my paygrade. And I'll go find the key." He looked around at the mannequins. "I gotta clean up this art project, too."

I tried one of the Sears doors one more time. "I'm worried about him, is all." But I also didn't want to get my own manager mad.

Jimmy found some compassion. "Tell you what, you work at Dillard's, right? I'll swing by in the morning to give you an update."

We walked carefully back through the crowd of mannequins, and that was the last time we saw Jimmy.

8

HANK MET me at Dillard's at the end of our shifts.

"Should we go check on Jimmy?" I suggested.

But instead we drove home.

As we pulled into the driveway, I finally got my question out. "What happened when I couldn't find you?"

But he just pointed at our daughter's car, already parked. "Marissa and the baby are home early."

I gave him a reprieve, but I wasn't letting this go.

We parked and walked inside to the smell of frying southwestern chicken.

Hank sniffed the air. "Nice to come home to that."

I tried not to be offended. He came home to a hot dinner on the days he worked and I didn't. He did the same for me on his days off. This wasn't an insult and I would choose not to take it that way.

Except.

He acted so much more excited, so much more grateful, when Marissa made us dinner.

"Smells great!" Hank told her, as Jake toddled up to me, arms outstretched.

The little guy was happy to have someone to pick him up, since Marissa had been cooking.

I tried to lose myself in playing with my grandson, but I was agitated. Jake had to keep grabbing my chin to point my face at the toys.

Those mannequins had to have been mechanical. Someone was filming a prank video to put on the internet.

But I was afraid this all meant that we should move with Marissa not to help take care of her and Jake, but so she could take care of us. After all, Hank and Jimmy had seen the strange mannequins, but only I'd seen them reach for me. Their movements might all be in my head.

"No," I said aloud. "Hank saw the first one move."

Jake grinned big, thinking he'd procured a reaction from me by smacking his blocks.

I laughed with him to encourage his growth. I was happy in my role.

If we moved into Marissa's new home, then would Jake grow up thinking of us as the dependent old folks who always needed help? Why would he ever come to me for advice if he thought I was a needy old lady?

Again, I felt little fingers redirect my chin. Jake needed help sliding a purple ring onto a yellow post. I did it for him.

He fussed at me.

"Well, use your words, then," I teased gently. "You have to tell me what you want."

Jake took the purple ring and placed it on top of two other rings he'd already stacked.

So that's what he'd wanted. I'd been assuming he was seeing things like I'd been.

A terrible thought occurred to me. I suddenly needed to ask Hank a question.

I picked up Jake and the purple ring to go back to kitchen.

I had to admit, dinner smelled really good.

Marissa sat on the counter, spatula in hand, while the chicken sautéed. She was telling Hank the plans she already had for boosting IT security at her upcoming new job. Hank nodded along. His computer degrees became obsolete a decade ago, and the stroke had slowed down his own processing power, but he probably followed more of it than I did.

I waited for Marissa to take a breath and then I interrupted. "Hank, that mannequin in the Sharper Image—it was moving, right?"

The confused look from my daughter didn't hurt as much as the concerned look from my husband.

Oh god. It hadn't been. It had all been in my head.

Jake slipped a few inches down my side as my body became heavy. Not only was something wrong with my brain, but now I'd declared as much to Hank and Marissa.

"The fingers pulled it forward," Hank said.

I'd never felt so relieved. I adjusted my arms to lift Jake up to shoulder level so he could play with my shirt collar.

"What are you guys talking about?" Marissa asked.

"Mannequins," Hank said. "Moving like robots."

No, their movement was smoother than robots', but I didn't say that. "I think someone's filming a prank show in the mall."

"That's bizarre." Marissa hopped down from the counter to flip the chicken breasts. "I wonder how they work."

Hank offered a guess, and my electronically-inclined family got lost in that discussion.

There in the kitchen, not part of the conversation but watching over them, I felt comfortable.

We had dinner and nobody brought up Marissa and Jake's upcoming move. It was the nicest evening we'd had as a family in a long time, if I ignored my worry about Saswin. Jimmy had said he'd call the police, so Saswin should be home safe by now.

That night in bed, Hank snored. I lay on my back looking up at the ceiling.

Within the darkness, I saw a steady pattern of movement like a gentle river or a well-oiled conveyer belt.

Or eight escalators, all going up to the second floor of the old Sears.

I rolled onto my side and went to sleep.

9

———

I HAD a nightmare that I was Saswin, wandering the empty mall. Dream logic had me believing that something sinister had closed down all these stores, and if I couldn't get them open and busy again, that sinister threat would turn its attention to me.

I awoke eager to get to work and hear from Jimmy that he'd found Saswin and delivered him safely to his daughter.

During the first half of my shift, as I took down the midweek sale posters and hung up the weekend sales, I kept looking to the doors to the mall. Despite his promise to update me, Jimmy never showed up.

So when I met Hank for lunch, I suggested we go knock on the door to the security office.

A man our age opened it. He saw my Dillard's name tag and Hank's Aunt Annie's vest and gave us a confused look. "Help you?"

"Is Jimmy around?"

He grunted a negative.

"He said he'd tell me what happened with my friend who walked into the old Sears yesterday. My friend is senile, used to work here."

"Didn't hear anything about it." The man shrugged and turned back to his desk. "Do y'all need anything else?"

We left him be.

"Let's go look in the Sears wing," I suggested.

"For what?" The harshness of Hank's response surprised me. He didn't want to go back there.

But I couldn't leave it alone. That nightmare of being inside Saswin's head was too on the nose. I hated the idea of my old friend not understanding where everyone had gone. "I'm worried," I told Hank. "Let's go check."

"The other guy said Jimmy's not in today." Hank said.

"I just want to see."

Hank relented.

We walked through the bright, empty mall corridor, past closed metal gates and dusty stores, to the branching hallway leading to the Sears wing.

As we came around the corner, the crowd of mannequins came into sight.

Twenty or so were in a pile by an unmarked beige door. Jimmy must have started gathering them to carry through the maintenance hallway and to the dumpsters out back.

But for some reason he'd stopped after barely making a dent.

Jimmy's pile seemed unnaturally *dense*, if that makes

sense. The stiff arms and legs of the mannequins should have prevented them from piling up so tightly.

The closer I inspected then, the more strangeness I saw. Yes, there were mannequins with extra limbs. And yes, there were mannequins with bits of the mall stuck into their bodies—green plastic ferns, flecks of shattered pastel tile, bright red fire alarms.

But the strangeness in Jimmy's pile of mannequins went beyond what I'd already seen. Several mannequins had sunk into each other. One's right leg now occupied the same space as another's torso. One's hand and head disappeared into another's back.

I didn't remember seeing any merged mannequins yesterday when we'd traversed the crowd.

My gut said something weird was progressing, that these mannequins hadn't simply arrived—they'd arrived with a purpose.

But rationality assured me that the pranksters had added the merged plastic figures overnight.

Hank interrupted my internal debate. "The mannequins are looking at us."

Except that wasn't quite right.

They all stared at the gap in the edge of the crowd, next to the conglomerating pile of plastic people.

My gut knew that empty space was where Jimmy had been working when they'd all turned to face him.

Swallowing my fear, I stepped into the semi-circle gap at the edge of the crowd. A hundred mannequins were pointing their eyeless faces at me.

Hank stayed behind, kicking at the haphazard pile.

"Jimmy started cleaning up," I said, "but he didn't do much." The bigger question was did he call the police before he left? Did they find Saswin? Did my old friend get home safe and sound?

"Maybe his shift ended," Hank suggested. "We could go back and ask how long he stayed yesterday."

I shook my head. "He said he'd be working until late. But whoever's got them wired up made them all look at Jimmy. Probably freaked him out so he got scared and left. That might mean he never called the police and I just left Saswin to wander the mall confused and alone."

I shouldn't have left it to someone else. I'm the one who protects my own. If Saswin got hurt last night, it was my fault.

"I'm sure Jimmy called." Hank let his gaze sweep across the crowd. "They're creepy, aren't they?" I saw him withdraw into himself.

Hank's fear surprised me. Last night he'd be hypothesizing with Marissa about how the electronic motors could work. I'd nearly convinced myself it'd make me a senile old biddy if I believed anything else, and now Hank was the one getting nervous.

"They give you the willies, that's for sure," I agreed, trying to keep him from feeling weak. I did a lot of that lately. Often, protecting someone meant protecting them from their own self-doubt.

"How could an internet prankster get so many mannequins?" he asked.

"You think it might be something else?"

Here's the thing: if Hank was entertaining the possibility that we were dealing with something other than teenagers with too much time on their hands, then that made it way more difficult for me to squash down that fear myself.

I tried to imagine the pranksters hurrying around the Sears wing, adjusting the crowd of mannequins to all fan out and point at the empty semi-circle. It didn't feel likely.

But more likely than mannequins magically deciding to walk around on their own? I couldn't say.

"We should leave," Hank said.

"Not yet. We don't know if Jimmy checked inside Sears."

"I don't want to be in here anymore." His voice cracked.

I'd only seen him this scared after his own confused episodes, when the anger wore off and he was left unsure of where the last five minutes had gone. Something had spooked him yesterday.

I looked down the hallway, through the crowd, to the Sears sign far at the end. I pictured those eight escalators, all going up. "If it's unlocked, I'd like to take a quick look around."

"No. You'd have to walk through the mannequins to get there." Hank hadn't looked away from the crowd.

His fear infected me.

It should be simple to believe it was all caused by pranksters with a talent for electronics, but there was too much I couldn't explain.

The strangest part being why all this should appear at the same time as Saswin.

The only reason I found the two mannequins was because I went into the Sears wing. But *nobody* goes down there. The only reason I did was because I heard Saswin singing. It was almost like Saswin lured me back there. Except, of course, Saswin wasn't mentally aware enough to play a prank.

So could we really conclude that some maliciously playful mechanical engineer just so happened to set up his robotic mannequins the exact same hour that a senile old man wandered back to his old place of employment?

I didn't buy it.

But how else could I explain it? I mean, without calling my own mental acuity into question. And with Marissa ready to move away to start a new life, now was not the time to broadcast doubt about Mom's brain.

Hank walked to my side.

Even though I stood in the gap Jimmy had made, and all the mannequins stared right at me, and Hank was more terrified than he'd ever admitted being, Hank walked to my side.

Thirty years of marriage, even after a stroke, he was constantly reminding me why I loved him.

"You okay?" he asked.

I took a breath. I wanted to check the Sears doors, but I couldn't possibly ask Hank to come with me. And not just out of compassion—too much stress might trigger an episode.

"I'll ask the other security guard to check. Let's get going."

As we left, I noticed two mannequins at the near edge of the crowd, merged together hip-to-hip.

10

———

I CLEANED up the women's sweaters after a young mother lost control of her toddlers, and then I refolded the women's blue jeans after a pair of choosy ladies inspected them all.

During my fifteen, I looked up the police non-emergency number. I'm not quick on the internet, but I can fumble my way around.

I dialed and asked if anyone had called about a senile man needing help at Cloverleaf Mall yesterday. There weren't any reports about it, but they told me it's possible a caller would be redirected to Adult Protective Services. I called that number but got a voicemail with instructions to call 911 if there was an emergency.

I escaped that bureaucratic loop by hanging up.

Back on the store floor, after ringing up the rare line of customers, I asked Helen if she still had Saswin's contact info.

"No, and I couldn't give it to you if I did. Against policy."

She'd never been the most helpful boss.

"But I can't stop you from looking him up on Facebook or Instagram or wherever."

"My daughter has Facebook. I'll get her help this evening."

"You don't wanna wait. Facebook's easy. Let me see your phone." Sometimes, Helen had her moments.

She helped me download the app and make an account. We searched "Saswin Patel" which brought up thousands of results.

We tried his daughter instead.

We scrolled through the more manageable number of people with the name "Sarah Patel." We found one that listed Virginia as her home state, and although the photo was tiny on my phone screen, I thought she might be the young woman who'd picked Saswin up from work those last few months before he retired.

I tapped "Add Friend" and sent a message, saying that I thought I'd seen her dad the other day and asking how he was.

"She won't see it unless she accepts your friend request," Helen said.

I actually knew that little factoid already. After we helped Marissa move back in, away from her ex, Hank had messaged the young man some legally actionable threats. When he calmed down, he got concerned, but Marissa had explained that her ex wouldn't see the messages anyways.

I recounted the story to Helen and we laughed.

It could be funny now that Marissa was no longer in danger.

Paul exiting our lives made the past feel distant.

Any big life change did the same.

It allowed you to laugh about old fears, but it also pushed away the good moments.

If we left our home and our city and my career to move north with Marissa, it'd put up a similar wall between us and everything we'd ever been.

It'd tie off this thread of our lives to start a new one. And who would I be in this new thread?

On my phone screen, my message to Saswin's daughter glowed unanswered.

11

AT THE END of the day, I walked back toward the food court. Hank had texted me that he was working an extra half-hour, so I had some time to kill.

I paused at the intersection leading to the Sears wing.

I listened for Saswin's playful song that I'd heard yesterday: "Close the blade before you pocket it."

But the mall speakers played a string-quartet version of "You Make My Dreams Come True" and the violin high notes were making the old speakers pop. I wouldn't have heard Saswin even if he was singing right around the corner.

Yesterday, music had been playing, too. So how had I heard him? Especially since he'd turned out to be so far down the hallway.

This was too much. I needed to go sit in the food court, wait for Hank to finish his shift, and then go home and wait for Saswin's daughter to respond and tell me that he'd made it home okay.

But.

I still hadn't checked the door to Sears. If Jimmy had unlocked it before he took off, maybe I could slip in and at least reassure myself that Saswin wasn't still in there.

And I wanted to see what was inside. There shouldn't have been that many escalators side-by-side; I wanted to know what I'd really seen.

I walked back around the corner.

The mannequins were as we'd left them this morning: the crowd stretching across the Sears wing but growing thicker down this way, all of them facing the gap where Jimmy had started tidying up.

The pile was still there as well, with some of the mannequins merging into each other. In fact, as I looked closer, I realized that all of them were now connected. Wrists disappeared into heads, legs ended where plastic stomachs began.

I looked closer at the rest of the crowd.

Multiple conglomerations were forming. Next to the dry, decorative fountain, four mannequins—or maybe five?—were frozen in the process of merging into a mass of shiny, white plastic. They'd brought in a wooden bench as well, which stuck out like a foreign growth.

Another conglomeration had formed by the old dress shop, and another way back near the Sears.

It'd only been four hours since I'd been here last. How had they changed so much?

It didn't matter.

I told myself that the engineer pranksters must have swapped them out again. I ignored how hollow that lie was starting to sound.

I needed to get to the far side to see if the Sears doors were unlocked.

Yesterday, I'd walked through the gauntlet with Hank and Jimmy. Yesterday, the mannequins hadn't been smashing themselves into each other, forming big masses of squished plastic.

Fear crawled up inside me.

I should wait for Hank.

But I couldn't leave Saswin behind.

Wait, that last thought didn't make sense.

I wanted to make sure Saswin hadn't stayed in the Sears. But if I waited for Hank to join me, how would that mean "leaving Saswin behind?"

And yet, I had an overwhelming feeling that I needed to go in there after Saswin right now or I'd be abandoning him.

The thought didn't feel like mine.

Blaming someone else for my thoughts certainly wasn't a sign of sharp thinking.

I'd had a strange thought, that was all.

I'd come here to check the Sears doors, and that's what I was going to do.

The crowd of mannequins staring at me was still creepy. But when people were in need, I looked after them. That's who I'd always been and it wasn't changing now.

These strange mannequins were all a dumb prank. Right now, the pranksters were likely watching me via camera, waiting for me to turn around so they could press a button and move all the mannequins forward an inch.

In fact, I'd prove it.

Standing in Jimmy's empty space, I turned my back on the crowd of mannequins.

My squashed-down fear exploded into terror—not my own feelings but terror forced into me by something else. It was so strong, so unique in flavor that I knew with certainty I was feeling someone else's emotions. They braided themselves into my own feelings and suddenly I needed to flee as instinctually as a mouse from an owl.

I started to whirl back around to face the mannequins, but I was too late.

A cacophony of plastic scraped against tile. Dozens of hard, smooth hands grabbed me from behind.

12

ALL UP AND down my legs, my arms, my neck—the iron grip of plastic fingers.

The world withdrew until there was only my body and the mannequin hands squeezing into my skin.

This couldn't be happening.

I needed to get away, get back to Hank, get back home to my family, away from this nightmare Sears wing.

I pulled away with all my strength but the mannequins held me tight.

These weren't robotics. There was no engineer prankster watching through a camera. These mannequin fingers moved too smoothly to be operated by remote control.

And I wasn't crazy. I wasn't hallucinating the pain as one mannequin hand missed grabbing my whole arm and instead clamped down on skin alone.

My stomach flipped and the mall stretched around me, which I attributed to adrenaline and fear.

I had to break free.

They only moved when I couldn't see them.

I tried to turn my head to look straight at the mannequins. Plastic hands gripped my neck, my cheeks, my hair, keeping me from turning around.

I could look nowhere but straight ahead while they held me tight.

The mall stretched farther still. The doors of the JCPenney were twenty feet away from me—now thirty, now sixty, still receding. Unless my mind had truly snapped, this was really happening. The mall itself was expanding.

The Borders bookstore on my right retreated on a path perpendicular to the JCPenney. To my left, an empty kiosk was riding the extending tile floor in the opposite direction from the closed bookstore. The empty fountain and benches rode alongside it.

Hundreds of yards beyond them, shuttered stores led the charge away from me.

I struggled against the mannequin's tight hands. I was only a few feet into the Sears wing and yet I was so far away from Hank and Marissa.

An empty field of tile flooring surrounded me.

The mannequins were doing this.

I didn't how or what it meant but I knew it was their doing. If I could only break free of their grasp, maybe the mall would snap back into place.

I tried to wrestle away but my strength wasn't what it used to be.

Behind me came the sound of plastic scraping on tile, plastic scraping on plastic. The mannequins were moving again, readying for something.

Again, a foreign impulse creeped inside me, but this time it wasn't warning me not to leave Saswin behind. Instead, it was a burst of grief—for what the mannequins were about to do to me and how that meant I'd be leaving everybody behind.

I added my own emotions to this mental invader, my own refusal to roll over. I'd taught my daughter via example to never give up.

I wouldn't let the mannequins do this to me.

But I didn't have the strength to pry them off. I'd already established that.

I went limp.

Their hands had been holding me back, stopping me from fleeing in any direction. But they weren't positioned to hold me up.

I tried to collapse straight down but one mannequin hand kept its grip. I toppled sideways and my hip struck the tile.

Pain shot up my side and down my leg but I ignored it enough to turn my neck and lock the mannequins in place with my gaze.

Every mannequin in the Sears wing had gathered in a tight semi-circle behind where they'd caught me. They were gathering together even more now, slim mannequins becoming masses of conjoined plastic. And what would happen once they all became one?

It didn't matter because I'd trapped them in place now.

I was free. I could limp out of here and back to Hank.

But when I'd broken free from the mannequins, the mall didn't snap back to normal.

It was still a desert of tiled floor, pastel patterns now the only interruption of the wide, open space. The dry fountain was now a thousand feet from me. The small shops that had been thirty feet away now barely visible.

In the distance, miles away, I could see the white vinyl letters of the JCPenney sign. From this far, they looked tiny.

I had no choice but to start walking.

13

———————

I opted for a sideways gait.

The mannequins would follow me if I didn't keep an eye on them, and walking backwards carried with it too high a risk of falling on my tailbone. I was lucky that my hip hadn't shattered already. My bones might not survive another collision with the tile.

But my bigger concern was looking too closely at the monstrosities the crowd of mannequins was becoming. The dense crowd had morphed into a dozen isolated patches of plastic, each a centralized mass of smooth trenches and pointy spikes, surrounded by mannequins still maintaining their individuality. Each huddle of mannequins was connected to their central mass through strings of plastic that hung like syrup.

The longer I let my gaze explore those horrors, the easier it was to convince myself that my mind had slipped away, and if I were to sit down and close my eyes, maybe

I'd find myself in a hospital bed, waking up to a new life of being cared for by my family.

And so I walked sideways, keeping the mannequins in my periphery as I put distance between us.

It was like someone had crossed Cloverleaf Mall with the Great Plains. The mall had stopped stretching, but JCPenney was already so far away that if I held out my arm I could cover up the whole storefront with my thumb.

I heard plastic sliding on tile and quickly looked back at the mannequins. I'd spent too long squinting at the exit.

The spread-out mannequin monstrosities had advanced and formed a tighter shape, so the crowd now appeared more like a misshapen arrow aiming at my heart.

I picked up my sideways walk again, aiming straight for the short hallway back to the mall's main drag. At least, I hoped I was. It was hard to be sure I was heading in the exact right direction when I didn't dare look that way.

I put another minute of walking between me and the mannequins and then I quickly checked on the path in front of me.

I whipped my head back around just as those scraping footsteps started again. The mannequins were all dead still, albeit closer.

I was playing a high-stakes game of Red Light, Green Light.

Worse, I had veered off course. The JCPenney sign was now off to the left. I was aimed at a smaller store at the end of the Sears wing.

I wasn't sure which store—I couldn't tell from this far away.

When I tried to spot the JCPenney sign again, I couldn't. Was that it, thick white lettering above dark rectangles that might be doors? Or was it over to the side, where there was more white lettering?

This shouldn't be that difficult. The closed anchor store was offset from all the little shops. But I was trying to spot it from miles away. My depth perception wasn't that precise anymore.

I told myself it didn't matter. I knew the exit was by one of those white vinyl signs. I'd walk in that direction until they grew clearer.

But after another five-minute stretch of walking, when I risked another glance, I now saw a third similar sign, this one off to the right.

I didn't know which was my way out.

Panic tried to well up inside me.

My calves grew tight.

Hank and I walked five times per week, but my legs weren't cut out for this.

This couldn't be happening. A desert had sprung up around me when the mannequins had grabbed hold. A desert made of Cloverleaf Mall. I was so isolated in the middle of these great plains of tile that I couldn't even decipher the familiar store signs.

Footsteps behind me.

I whipped my head back around but this sideways walking had me off balance. My feet tangled and I fell.

My wits stayed about me enough that I both went limp to avoid striking any single bone too hard, and I kept my eyes pointed at my pursuers.

The nearest blob of mannequin was frozen only ten feet away.

I pushed myself back up from the cold tile floor.

Walking sideways might not be any better than walking backwards. Although if I'd fallen on my tailbone rather than onto my side, it wouldn't matter which way the exit was—I wouldn't be going anywhere.

I walked sideways away from the mannequins, no longer with any idea of my destination. I only knew I didn't want that mass of plastic and its linked mannequins to grab me and push the world even farther away.

Again, I made a rapid search for the white vinyl sign. But now I saw a fourth and fifth possibility. When I'd fallen, I don't think I faced the right direction upon standing up. I might even be walking toward the Sears, for all I knew.

All around me, miles of empty mall surrounded by shuttered stores.

I couldn't let panic take over because I couldn't risk moving quickly. I had to stay slow and in control.

If I could make it to any store, then I could follow them around the outside of this impossible mall desert to reach the exit.

I'd keep on walking—sideways, as goofy as it felt—in the direction that felt best.

What else could I do?

Enough time passed that the ache in my calves spread to my hamstrings. My neck got stiff from staring sideways at the mannequins.

Ten minutes, thirty minutes, longer.

Each step on the tile hurt my heels.

The mannequins watched me from the middle distance.

I took another glance behind me. The stores were closer now, but still not clear enough to read their signs.

I quickly looked back at the mannequins. Closer, but not close. Despite the space I'd put between us, I waited another three minutes before looking away again.

I still only saw a thin line of shops, sandwiched between the ceiling above and floor below.

But now I could just barely make out the signs above two of them: a knives and collectibles store and an Old Navy.

Those were halfway down the hallway to Sears. I'd really got myself turned around.

I guessed again at the right direction and headed off.

Depression sank in. My legs hurt so badly.

Someone called my name, distant, garbled.

Did this fake desert have auditory mirages?

They called again. This time I was listening.

It was Hank!

I'd been lost for so long that his shift had ended and he'd come looking for me. I'd never been so happy to hear his voice.

"I'm here!" I called back. "Where are you?"

He yelled again, and this time I pinpointed where it came from. Back toward the Old Navy.

That couldn't be right. Shouldn't he have entered the Sears wing and seen this massive expanse? Wouldn't he be yelling from the JCPenney? I didn't care. "Keep talking!" I shouted. "I'm heading for you."

Was he in this endless plain of tile? Was he somehow outside it?

"This way!" he called.

Whatever he was seeing, he wasn't wasting time asking about the reality of it all. He was guiding me.

I followed his voice.

Five minutes, ten minutes, thirty.

His calls of, "This way," grew more raspy.

The Old Navy and knife store, gated and empty though they were, came into clearer view and I loved the sight of them.

Hank's voice stayed the same volume the whole way.

I took a painful step no different from the rest and the mall snapped back into place. The wall of stores rushed at me like a train. Air pressure tightened. Just as I thought the metal gate over the Old Navy was going to pass through me and slice me into little cubes, it all came to a stop, right where it belonged.

Hank stood in front of the knife shop. He suddenly noticed me as if I'd popped out of thin air.

My husband pulled me into an embrace. I felt closed in by his body and I sank into that feeling.

14

———————

I STAYED in my Hank's arms. I felt him hold me close and look over my shoulder, keeping his eyes on the mannequins.

"What are they?" he asked.

My fear of losing my mind slipped away. He was seeing the conjoining mannequin masses. He knew he had to keep looking at them to hold them still.

But despite that relief, my heart still raced. My mind tried to pull me in a million directions at once. None of this could be real. I had to get home and never come back to Cloverleaf. I had to find Saswin and get him out of here.

"How far away did they leave you?" Hank asked.

I pulled away from his chest to look into his eyes. His fear suddenly made sense. Yesterday, I'd lost sight of him in the crowd as we followed Jimmy to the Sears. When he'd reappeared, he looked shaken. "It happened to you too," I realized aloud.

Hank nodded. "I thought it might be in my head. But I guess not."

"How long did you have to walk to get away?" I asked Hank.

"Too long," he answered. "One of them grabbed me, and then, all the stores were twenty or so feet away. I broke free and walked back to you."

"I was stuck for what felt like hours," I said. "Ten of them grabbed me and the whole world shot away."

Hank squeezed me tighter. "Not me," he said. "I'm still here. I found you."

I relaxed into the familiar safety of his arms. Of course, there was a limit to that feeling of safety, considering our circumstances.

I turned around, leaning back against my husband.

With the mall shrunk down to its normal size, the horrific blobs of plastic limbs felt so much more threatening. The still-independent mannequins that were leashed to each blob stared mournfully at me. I thought maybe there were fewer individual bodies now, those drooping strands of plastic made shorter until another mannequin was absorbed.

Had they wanted to submerge me into their flesh as well? Was that the sense of impending intention that I'd felt before I wiggled free?

One of the blobs was half inside the empty fountain. I suspected that once it moved again, it would bring the cement ornaments with it. Another had already gathered a row of gumball machines, their bright red metal sticking out from its white plastic surface.

I stood straight. "Should we call the police?"

"And tell them what?" Hank asked.

"I don't know." After my earlier 9-1-1 call, I wasn't sure who would answer the phone if we called again.

"I don't know what they are," said Hank, "but we should get out of here."

I swallowed my fear. "Not until we find Saswin."

"Lisa," Hank said with annoying patience. "You barely survived."

"I'm fine."

"Jimmy's not."

In those two words, I instantly understood everything he was saying. We'd both seen the semicircle of mannequins this morning around the empty spot where Jimmy had been piling them up. How long had they let him toss them into the corner before they pounced? "They took Jimmy. Pushed away the world. He never found his way out."

The only way I'd escaped was because Hank had called for me.

I sucked in a breath and yelled for Jimmy, screamed his name at the mannequins and masses of mannequin flesh that watched me silently.

"He's gone," Hank said. "It's been too long."

"How do you know?"

"I can feel it. Can't you?"

He was right. There was no helping Jimmy. And it was

my fault. Except, what would I have done differently? Ignore Saswin's lonely cries? I couldn't ignore him yesterday and I wouldn't today.

"We can still help Saswin," I said to Hank.

"No. We're going home."

Throughout our marriage, I'd always bristled when he tried to put his foot down with me. But since his stroke, I'd come to appreciate these moments of self-assuredness.

But appreciating and obeying were two different things.

"I'm not leaving until I look for him."

"Can you even walk?"

I evaluated myself. My hip hurt from my fall. The soles of my feet hurt from walking on the tile for so long. The muscles in my legs ached, but I wasn't out of juice yet. "Of course I can. We're not leaving without looking for Saswin."

Hank squeezed my hand. His fingers trembled.

What I'd taken for stoic bravery was the exact opposite. He'd barely been holding his fear at bay.

"We have to," I said gently, as if my fear were any less. "I can't leave Saswin behind."

Was that my thought or some foreign intruder? I didn't know.

Hank nodded. "I'll go with you. Easier to trap the mannequins with two sets of eyes."

Before I could think better of it, I led the way around the outer edge of the Sears wing. We both walked sideways, keeping watch on the mannequin blobs and their leashed followers.

A kiosk cut off our line of site to one monstrosity. Plastic scraped on tile until the thing came into sight again, now a different assortment of shapes and also missing one of its leashed mannequins.

"What if Sears is still locked?" Hank whispered.

I didn't know so I didn't answer.

But when we reached the doors at the end of the hall-way, with their beige paper blocking the view through the glass, they opened without resistance.

15

———

As I PUSHED OPEN the door, warm air seeped out from the old Sears.

"What do you see?" asked Hank, facing the mannequins which waited to pursue us.

"Escalators," I said.

And that's all there was to see: eight escalators facing the doors. They had power going to them, and they were on, moving up. The rest of the department store was totally empty. Not even a loose hanger left behind. Evening light came through two papered-over vestibules.

The escalators rose slowly toward a black opening in the ceiling.

Hank risked a glance. "When did they build those?"

"I don't think anyone did."

"Maybe not," agreed Hank. "You think Saswin went up there?"

Somehow I was sure that he did.

We walked in, Hank letting the door shut behind us. We waited a few moments to see if the mannequins tried to open the doors, but the coast seemed clear.

I peered around the store. Totally empty like this, it looked bigger than the Dillard's. The light from the two vestibules was just enough to catch the dust in the air. We could easily see that Saswin wasn't down here.

The eight escalators beckoned us to explore above.

I started walking.

"Hold on," Hank said. "Are we really going up there? Do you have a flashlight?"

"Our phones do."

We reached the bottom of the escalators and pulled out our phones. I couldn't find the app, but I told Siri to turn it on and she did.

"Ready?" I asked Hank.

He shook his head, but he stepped onto the escalator first. Perhaps a chivalrous way to keep me safe, or perhaps so I could catch him if he stumbled backwards.

The machinery hummed beneath our feet as we ascended. We drew closer to the black space in the ceiling where the escalators ended.

It was like the inverse of when the mannequins grabbed me. Instead of the world fleeing, I was approaching the world. I wasn't sure what that thought meant. It felt injected.

I suddenly grew scared that if my thoughts weren't my own, was something luring me upstairs? Or was this what I really wanted to do?

The escalator carried us closer to the blackness above.

Hank shrunk into himself. I touched his back. Reassurance for both of us.

The lights from our phones pushed into the dark as we rose.

Hank broke the surface of the shadow and the parts of me that felt both protective and powerless worried that he would disappear, as if the shadow were a black ocean.

But my flashlight kept him visible. I broke the plane of shadow behind my husband. And then his shoes tapped on the metal at the top of the escalator as he walked onto the second floor.

I closed my hand around the fabric of his shirt, suddenly afraid that we would get separated. I reached the top of the escalator and walked off behind him.

Upstairs felt as empty as down below, but I really couldn't be sure. Our phone lights weren't made for distance—they spread wide instead of reaching far.

The floor at our feet was the same tile as downstairs. There were tile pathways with islands of carpet. Clothing, bedding, and housewares had been up here before Sears closed.

I didn't know where to look for Saswin.

The dark openness around us tugged at my nerves. I wanted to retreat home, clear my head, and try to understand what was happening with the mannequins. But I had to help Saswin right now.

Except, did I?

Why did that impulse feel so foreign, like someone had implanted the thought?

"Where do you want to check?" Hank asked.

"Any place is as good as the next," I said.

He heard my uncertainty and stepped up. "Let's walk straight ahead, find the wall, then circle the room."

"Do you think we can find our way back downstairs?" I asked.

Hank pointed his light behind us, which wasn't necessary, since the sunlight coming through the doors downstairs glowed faintly up the escalators.

In this dark, open second floor, the bank of eight escalators was a faint beacon right in the middle.

"And don't worry about getting down," Hank kicked at a clear plastic box on the floor. There was a red button inside. "We can stop them whenever we want."

I appreciated his calm problem-solving, despite his fear.

Of course, since the stroke, everything he said was slow and measured, so he sounded calm even when he was furious. Or even when he was terrified.

Before we started into the dark, Hank offered me his elbow like a teenager at the senior prom. I took it, leaning into my husband, ready to search the darkness so my old friend wouldn't think he'd been left behind.

16

———

WHEN WE'D WALKED FAR ENOUGH into the dark that our flashlights could no longer illuminate the path back to the escalators, that's when Hank had an episode.

His body went stiff. I put one hand on his chest and the other behind his arm, ready to balance him if he started to tip. "You okay?"

With my flashlight smothered against Hank's chest, and his at his side, the shadow of the upstairs infected the contours of my husband's face. He stared through me.

I didn't remember exactly how it worked, but something in his brain wasn't connecting with something else, and instead of just having a hard time putting his thoughts into words, he was having a hard time actually making his thoughts.

I needed to get him home, or at least to the car where he could sit down and take a breath until things reconnected again. Saswin would have to wait. "Time to go," I cooed.

But just as I got us turned around, I heard it again, Saswin singing his silly rhyme: "Close the knife before you pocket it."

I whipped my head around, pinpointing where it had come from.

Saswin was still here. The poor man had been here since yesterday. Had he slept on the tile? How hungry must he be? Where was he relieving himself?

I pointed my phone's light around the dark, but it only reached a few feet.

"Saswin?" I called. He didn't answer.

Hank didn't ask why I was yelling. He didn't say anything.

Hank wasn't a medical risk at this moment. These episodes were scary, but not dangerous. So I held his hand tight and led him farther away from the escalators toward where I'd heard Saswin singing.

"Are you over here?" I called into the dark.

We reached the wall. I yelled for my friend again, but no answer.

I pointed my light along the drywall. Scuffs and scrapes and cracked posters of ten dollars off crockpots.

"Saswin?"

No answer.

The corner of the sales floor came into view, which surprised me because I didn't think we'd walked far enough yet.

With a gentle tug on Hank's hand, I started toward that corner. Hank let out an uncomfortable groan. I stopped walking.

"I'm sorry. Did you get hurt?"

These episodes weren't harmful in themselves, but if something was hurting Hank, he wouldn't be able to tell me.

"We'll go back. I'm sorry. We'll go back."

But again, Saswin's song came from up ahead. "Close the knife before you pocket it."

And so I told Hank, "Let's just make a circle. We'll check for Saswin and then go home."

We reached the corner of the sales floor to find the entrance to a dark hallway.

When the Sears had been open, had this been offices? Or maybe the family photo studio? I couldn't remember.

"Saswin?"

No answer. A closed-in hallway might be the most comfortable place to sit down, if Saswin had been in here lost and confused.

I led Hank inside.

Only a few steps down the hallway, and it turned. As I made that turn, a sudden bright light made me squint.

Hank raised a hand over his eyes. How could it be so bright back here, when we hadn't seen anything until we turned the corner?

As my eyes adjusted, I saw another wing of the mall, packed full of everything but people.

17

───────────

IT WAS the mall I'd known for twenty years, but also a place I'd never seen before. Shops and kiosks and pastel patterns on the walls and tile floor.

This couldn't exist. It didn't exist. For one, we were upstairs. The anchor stores all had a second floor, but the mall itself did not.

And this place didn't look right regardless. The hallway was too narrow, the shops facing each other were too close together. The ceiling was too low, no higher than the eight-foot ceilings in our own home.

Despite the tight space, all of what you'd expect in a shopping mall was jammed inside. A bench was half in and half out of an operating decorative fountain. Water trickled out of the spout, making its way back to the bright blue pool. Pennies and nickels and quarters filled that pool near to the top, breaching the water's surface in little hills.

Kiosks were on top of each other, one with cell phones, another with toy dogs yipping and whirring as they walked in robotic motions. Another kiosk held trading cards and yet another displayed jewelry.

All of these sat tail-to-nose, splitting the hallway down the middle. The walkways between the kiosks and the storefronts weren't wide enough for me and Hank to walk side-by-side. I didn't recognize a single store name although the logos were almost familiar.

A clothing store aimed at teens was called Southwest Bluebird. Clothes on hangers were stacked on top of the racks in great piles up to the ceiling. Although the shop gate was open, the piles of clothes formed a vertical wall at the front of the store, as if pressed up against glass. A walkway like a small slot canyon led into the great stacks of clothes. It curved out of sight.

Across from Southwest Bluebird was a red and yellow store sign for Toys By KayDee. Toys filled the shop, burying most of the shelves. Board games piled on top of Barbies on top of video game consoles. Another slot canyon led inside.

Next door was a candy shop. All the surplus candy pressed against an invisible barrier, reminding me of a candy store glass counter if every single cubic inch had been shoved full.

Next to that, a men's clothing store. And across from that, a shop selling puzzles and calendars, and a dark and neon shop with offensive t-shirts and gag-gifts. In each, merchandise filled the space as if it'd been delivered by dump truck. And in each, that merchandise stayed within the store boundaries, pressed up against invisible barriers.

The lights in the too-low ceiling were garish and bright, as if they were the proper brightness for a thirty-foot ceiling, but were now shining at me from two feet above my head.

I squeezed Hank's hand to both offer and receive emotional support. "What is this place?"

His wide eyes and open mouth told me he didn't know but he didn't like it. He stepped back towards the darkness behind us. I noted that his episode might be on its way out if he could understand my questions.

"Yeah," I agreed, "we should go."

And then once again, Saswin's song came from down the hall. "Close the knife before you pocket it."

I couldn't tell quite how far this hallway went. Maybe not more than five or six stores, but the tight kiosks and low ceiling made it hard to be sure.

Saswin's voice hadn't been that far away. Close enough to go find him again.

I tried not to imagine how he would feel, being lost in here, not understanding why he was alone, why he'd been left behind.

"Come on," I said to Hank. "We can go find Saswin and then head right back out."

Hank was no longer looking at me. He was staring into the toy store, down into the canyon, between walls of toys that led inside. If his brain was working right, he'd tell me that this place wasn't safe, that it wasn't part of the mall at all, that we might be stepping into a nightmare.

Hank's fear permeated me, as well. And with it, a venomous sadness that Saswin had spent all night alone in this unnatural place.

It was discomforting enough with Hank at my side. How much more terrible would it be if I were alone and I didn't know how I got here? If the last thing I remembered was that I was with my daughter, and if she wasn't here, then that must mean that she had left me in this place where there were too many toys, too many clothes, too much stuff without anyone to put it to use.

Hank stepped toward the exit.

"No," I insisted. "We have to get Saswin first. He's not getting left behind."

I pulled Hank forward before he could protest. We walked past the squeaking and whirring dogs. We reached the kiosks that had broken my line of sight so I could now see more of the hallway.

It was more of the same. Shops too close together filled to the ceiling with merchandise, each with paths disappearing inside.

And once again, down the hall was a crowd of kiosks blocking my view.

"Saswin!" I yelled, feeling more desperate the deeper we walked.

We had to keep going. But I was becoming very aware of how difficult it would be to flee out of here. Regardless of Hank's and my mobility, we'd have to squeeze past benches and gumball machines and store displays. The farther we went from the exit, the tighter we wedged ourselves in.

"Maybe we should head back," I admitted.

That same feeling of intrusive thoughts hit me again. This time, not a gut feeling but actual words:

Don't leave me here.

Either senility had snuck up on me, or Saswin was pushing his thoughts into mine.

It was beyond how I understood reality, but the thought of leaving him behind filled me with so much disgust that I didn't spare time to consider how strange and impossible this all was.

"I'm coming," I called. We kept walking, and as we passed more kiosks and more fountains and more benches and more stores, those invisible barriers in the shop entrances stopped working.

A pile of soaps and shampoos and lotions, all pastel colors and oozing sweet scents, impeded our path. We kicked our way through.

In front of the next shop, men's formal wear made up a thick rug that was actually a nice relief for aching heels.

After that, chocolates made our pathway slippery, but we leaned on each other to stay on our feet.

"Lisa." Hank's voice made me jump, even though he'd been right next to me this whole time. I didn't expect him to be able to speak for another half hour. His episode was clearing up quickly, which was good news for his overall recovery. But right now, his worried expression asked, *What are we doing?*

I couldn't admit that I'd heard Saswin's voice in my head. Instead, I said, "I heard him singing again."

Hank peered down the hallway. I knew he wanted to talk some sense into me. The place felt unnatural.

I took advantage of his limited speech to plow through with what I wanted. "We'll just check to the end of this wing."

If it ended.

We continued hand in hand, deeper into this lost hall-way, walking over clothes and CDs and perfume bottles. We leaned on each other for balance as the layers of merchandise grew deeper. The hallway floor became a valley with hills of *stuff* rising into the shops on either side.

As we trudged past another kiosk—this one covered in stacks of Pokémon cards—a strange view came into sight.

Those consumeristic hills on either side rose all the way to the low ceiling. Video game boxes and children's clothes stuck to that ceiling above our heads. Onward from here, the entire hallway was coated in four sides by items for sale that would never be sold.

It created an effect like a tunnel, or the entrance to a funnel spider's trap.

What we saw in front of us, however, was what really caught our attention.

"How?" Hank asked.

Before I could respond, my phone buzzed in my hand, a notification from Sarah Patel:

Dad lives with me in Seattle now. He's doing as well as you can hope. We're having a family movie night right now.

Saswin wasn't in the mall. He wasn't even on the East Coast.

And yet, in Cloverleaf Mall's lost hallway, at the entrance to this tunnel of merchandise that stretched on forever behind him, there stood Saswin.

18

———

"He's small." Hank pointed at my old friend.

Saswin wore his Dillard's uniform: khakis, a navy polo, and a name tag. He had his beard and mustache trimmed how he used to, and his hair was as dark as the day he started working, not the salt and pepper from when he retired.

But what Hank pointed out was accurate. Saswin was too small.

Some old folks shrink a bit as they age, but Saswin had taken it to a new level. He couldn't be taller than four feet now, despite maintaining all his proportions.

He stood sideways to us, hunched forward, eyes pointed to a pile of comic books by his feet.

"Saswin?" I asked, knowing it couldn't be him, that the real Saswin was safe with his daughter across the country.

He looked up but not at me. His brown eyes had a quivering sense of life to them. Without melody, he said, "Close the knife before you pocket it."

"Why did you say that?" I asked, fearing that the answer was because it would lure me here.

He seemed to notice me for the first time. His head popped up. He rubbed his hands in excited relief. "You're here. Where have you been?"

He reached down to his feet to scoop up an armful of Superman comics and lacy women's underwear. He offered them to me. "These are worth visiting for, right?"

I felt Hank's hand on my elbow. He was ready to pull me behind him. Hank hadn't seen the message from Saswin's daughter, but he knew as well as I did that something was wrong.

"Where did everyone go?" Saswin asked, jiggling his offering of comics and underwear.

When neither Hank nor I responded, the little Saswin scurried to another store.

Hank pulled me to the other side of the strange tunnel, giving the small man space.

Saswin scooped up an armful of body lotions and shampoos. He squeezed too tight and pink glittery goop plopped onto the baseball caps at his feet. "Everyone used to love this. They came, smelling wonderfully, and crowded in to pick even more wonderful smells. But where did they go?"

"This isn't Saswin," I said to Hank.

Hank shook his head. "No, I don't..." But he couldn't quite get out the rest of his thought.

He nudged me and pointed back past the kiosks, the way we'd come. I wasn't ready to go yet. This wasn't Saswin, but they still needed help. Whoever he was, I couldn't leave him behind.

"How long have you been here?" I asked.

The Saswin lookalike peered at me through his dully glowing eyes. "Always. The deer wore this trail into the grass and they rested in a thicket over there."

He pointed deeper into the tunnel.

"Then people used the trail. I liked them better. But they wore the grass down to dirt. Eventually, so many people came that they had to put stone down to walk on. Imagine that."

His head lolled about dreamily, happily.

"So many people that they brought stone from other places so they could walk near me. Not because of me, I know that. But how wonderful, anyways? They turned trees into structures, and came to visit and trade and exchange. And then this structure is so big, I'd never existed so concretely."

He clapped his hands, delighted at the sharp sound.

The tunnel of merchandise didn't allow an echo.

He looked me in the eyes for the first time. His brown irises looked normal, but the whites wavered between white and a cream color. "Thank you for coming to help. Tell me, where has everybody gone?"

I tried to process what he'd said, this person who looked like Saswin but a foot shorter. It wasn't him. This person was claiming to have been here before there were roads. Richmond had been around for almost 400 years. And how many centuries before that had there been paths down this intersection? How old was he claiming to be?

What was he? Some ancient spirit? A god of the land?

"Why do you look like my friend?" I asked.

He touched a finger to his mouth. *Shhhh.* "I look like who you most want to help."

I was taken aback. "No. If that were the case you'd look like my daughter or grandson. Or there'd be two Hanks here right now."

He winked. "You're here. I must have picked correctly."

No. Saswin was an old friend I'd lost touch with after his dementia. I was only here because I hated the idea of him feeling like he'd been left behind in the mall.

What was most important to me was my daughter becoming self-sufficient, my husband completing his recovery, my grandson growing up confident.

But what this god had said struck true deep in my gut, where I knew myself whether I thought about it or not.

Hank was well on his way to recovery. The brevity of this latest episode was proof of that.

And Marissa *was* self-sufficient. This new job was a big step up, but she was already there, really. She only lived with us for some extra family support while she recovered from her bad relationship.

And she was a great mom to Jake. If I never spoke to my grandson again, he'd still grow up strong and confident.

My family didn't need me to lead and guide anymore.

But that's what I did. It's who I was. And now Marissa was moving and Hank was recovering and now what?

But Saswin. I'd always helped Saswin.

He was nervous when he started the job. And the dementia came on slowly. I covered for him. When he got confused, I reminded him what he'd been doing.

I'd been so scared for him, so any little way I could help also assuaged my own fear.

Yesterday, when I thought he'd wandered back to the mall and he'd be confused why it was empty, why everyone had left him behind, of course I jumped in to help.

I didn't care if this god was Saswin or not. He'd been left behind. I helped people. That part about me hadn't changed. I wouldn't let it.

This thing who looked like Saswin scurried to the next shop door. He lifted a tuxedo jacket by the shoulders and held it up. "What about this? You like this, don't you?"

"Take it," I said to Hank.

He shook his head. "Don't get close." Protective like always.

But there wasn't anything to worry about here.

The Saswin-thing looked at me pleadingly. "Go get more people and bring them. Someone will like these things. It's what brought them before and it'll bring them again."

I wasn't sure about that. So much shopping was done on computers now.

Hank grabbed my elbow, harder this time.

"I'm not getting close to him," I said.

Hank pointed back down the hallway.

"We can't leave yet. I want to help him."

"Look," Hank insisted.

Hearing the fear in my husband's voice, I looked back where we'd come.

A blob of mannequin flesh, peppered with protruding limbs and mall detritus, blocked our escape.

19

———

Hank pushed me behind him.

The mannequin blob sat there frozen.

There were no more mannequins attached by plastic threads. They'd all been brought together, forming enough mass to fill this claustrophobic hallway from floor to ceiling and wall to wall.

The kiosk full of Pokémon cards had been half-absorbed by the blob. The cards had scattered over the surface, speckling the bright white plastic in little rectangles of color.

I scanned for a way past.

The mass of plastic had been coming straight up the middle. Its round shape left gaps in the corners of the hallway. I thought we could maybe fit through the gap on the bottom right. That is, if our knees could take it. And if we were willing to crawl through the forest of mannequin limbs that stuck out from the blob.

That wouldn't work, though. If we brushed against them, they'd push away the world.

I didn't have the energy for another long walk home.

"Oh," came Saswin's voice behind me. "I made those recently. A distraction from the emptiness. It didn't work."

Hank and I exchanged a glance, unsure how to respond. The Saswin-thing was looking past us at the mass of mannequin plastic. Then his gaze drifted to his own hands, and a wistful smile tugged at the corners of his mouth. "At first, I could create them perfectly. But now..."

His fingers twitched as if grasping for an ability he remembered possessing. His lips tightened as he focused. An eerie, pale light shone from his hands. He brought his palms together and the light intensified, seeping out between his fingers.

Hank took a cautious step back, pulling me with him. The Saswin-thing paid us no mind, lost in his own world as he slowly drew his hands apart. The light stretched and morphed between them.

I couldn't take my eyes away. The light struck me as even older than this man or god that stood before us.

The light flickered. It sparked a flickering rainbow. And then it took shape, forming a grotesque mass of fingers. The digits twitched and writhed as they floated between the Saswin-thing's hands.

He jerked back, disgusted by his work.

The spider-like ball of fingers fell, landed on the cardboard lid of a board game, and scuttled away, darting beneath a pile of men's dress shirts.

I couldn't tear my gaze from the spot where it had disappeared. My mind reeled with the memory of the mannequin head and arm that we'd seen in the Sharper Image. That felt like a lifetime ago.

The Saswin-thing wiped his hands on his slacks, a movement that I remembered the real Saswin doing. "I can't do it right anymore. Everything is slipping away."

He looked up again at the frozen plastic blob behind us, with its arms and legs sticking out so it looked like a magnified virus molecule. "Everything was already slipping away. Even the first ones have a mind of their own."

My brain made a connection and my protective side kicked on. "They took a security guard named Jimmy. Can you bring him back?"

He dug through piles of mall merchandise. He claimed to miss people so badly, but apparently he couldn't be bothered about Jimmy. I seethed.

"They didn't take him," the Saswin-thing said. "They pushed away the rest of the world. He'll have to walk back on his own."

"But what if it's too far?"

"Then he'll keep walking. If I know anything about people, it's that when you want to be somewhere, you can walk and walk and walk to get there."

"Can't you help? This is somebody still here in the mall. Don't you care about him?"

"Yes, I want him to stay."

"Then help him!"

"I can't."

"Then help me get to him."

"That's not necessary."

I hated that his loneliness didn't extend to compassion. "It darn well is necessary. How do I find him?"

"You can't. The world has been pushed away from him. There's no way in. Only out." He was insistent and I didn't understand enough of what was going on to keep arguing.

I was sick of problems with no solution.

If I couldn't find a way for Marissa to stay with us and still advance her career, then I should at least be able to help poor Jimmy. "What if I let the mannequins grab me? Will that take me where I can find him?"

Hank tapped my arm. "I think we can slip past."

He'd spotted the same narrow gap that I had.

"Unless it grabs us," Hank said.

"We'll keep looking at it." I wasn't sure it would work but I didn't know what else to do. I turned to the Saswin-thing. "If I let the mannequins grab me, can I get to Jimmy?"

He held up a black leather belt with a stripe of rhine-stones. "Do you like this?"

I gave him my best *assistant-store-manager* voice, which was the same as my *Mom* voice but with more threatening undertones. "Answer my question, please."

"I'll answer and you will stay." Not an offer or a command but a statement. "Letting the mannequins touch you would be foolish. They'll push away the world, including the spot where they pushed it away from Jimmy."

"Even if I go to the exact same spot where he was?"

"It wouldn't matter. When the world leaves you behind, it's quite personal."

I couldn't help Jimmy. I felt empty.

Into that emptiness flooded fear.

We were trapped in an impossible mall hallway, by a plastic monster, alongside an ancient god who'd gone insane with loneliness.

What had I dragged us into?

"Do you hear that?" Hank hissed.

From the far side of this mannequin blob, I heard plastic scraping on tile.

"There's another one back there," I realized aloud. We were even more boxed in.

I couldn't help the Saswin-thing, but maybe he could help us.

"How do we get past them?" I pleaded.

"You don't need to," the Saswin-thing said. "I answered your question so you won't leave."

My heart would have broken for this lonely god who only wanted his life to stay the same, but it was pounding too intensely at the fear of getting grabbed again. I couldn't go back to that desert of tile floors.

"Is that the only way through?" Hank pointed to the tiny space, where the roundish blob didn't reach the bottom corner of the hallway.

"Please," I asked the Saswin-thing. "We can't stay here. If we look away, that monster will come for us."

Saswin's eyes considered me with pity, but I quickly realized it was self-pity.

Hank took my hand in a firm grip and led me to the closest storefront. We climbed up a mountain of dolls, action figures, and video game cases until we were inside the shop.

The air felt different in here. Lighter, crisper.

"What are we doing?"

Hank struggled to get the words out. "Bait it this way. Then we go around. Close your eyes."

"I will not." I wouldn't let that thing isolate me again.

"Fine. I'll close mine first. You choose when to draw it close." Without a single doubt in me, Hank shut his eyes.

That left it up to me to lure the thing closer.

I almost told the Saswin-thing to look away, but I decided the rules of the mannequins likely didn't apply to him.

After one last look at the many-limbed mass of mannequin flesh, I squeezed my eyes shut. "One. Two."

Plastic scraped on tile.

"Three."

I opened my eyes to see a wall of plastic hands and fingers looming over me. I could've reached out to shake hands with the closest one.

Hank was looking too, now. "That was close."

We inched our way around the blob. As we did, I saw that the Saswin-thing was staring intently at its malformed creation.

Before I could think about what that meant, Hank led

me firmly to the far side of the hallway, over merchandise and through a much larger gap between the monster and the men's clothier.

Behind it, a smaller mannequin blob proved easy to navigate around.

The Saswin-thing wailed from behind us, "Please don't leave yet."

My heart ached with reblossoming pain on his behalf, but we fled toward the dark exit of this lost hallway.

At the escalators, Hank pressed the emergency stop button and we made it downstairs without difficulty.

The Sears wing was now empty of mannequins and their amalgamations.

I drove us home.

20

———

APART FROM THE insanity of all we'd faced in that lost hallway, something wasn't sitting right with me, but I couldn't put my finger on it. A question I wanted to ask but couldn't articulate quite yet.

Marissa had again made us dinner, but it was cold by the time we made it home. Jake was in bed.

I wanted to go to bed, too, or at least to the bedroom with Hank where we could talk privately about what we'd just witnessed.

I'd tried to talk in the car, saying that Saswin was still inside and shouldn't we help him? But Hank pointed out that the person we saw was not Saswin before telling me he needed to catch his breath. He didn't want to talk about it yet, which was his prerogative.

Now Hank sat in his rocking chair and listened to Marissa describe her plans for the big moving weekend.

Hank said that he and I were still considering Marissa's invitation.

To fill the air, I acknowledged that up in Fairfax, jobs were plentiful, and although I wouldn't be able to transfer within Dillard's, I could likely find another assistant manager retail job. Should we decide to move, that was.

Inside my head, I was growing frustrated with Hank. Why was he acting like everything was normal? There was a hallway in Cloverleaf Mall that couldn't be there, populated by mannequins which had squished themselves together, and a scared god that looked like my old coworker.

As I sat next to my daughter on the couch, I drifted in and out of listening to her because I wanted to lean my head back and weep for the confusion and loneliness that Saswin must be feeling. Or rather, the god that looked like Saswin.

Marissa walked us through her plan for packing boxes and arranging them in the garage to make loading the moving truck as efficient as possible. She'd make a fantastic retail manager, so I knew she was going to blow them away at her new career.

She asked if we were up for helping with the final packing, which was fine with me. My body was exhausted, but doing something active might calm my mind.

It didn't.

I packed Jake's board books in the box that Marissa had labeled *fantasy paperbacks*. I kept getting distracted, replaying in my mind Saswin's voice begging us not to leave.

I would have stayed to help him, obviously. I didn't want to leave anyone confused and lonely. Even discovering that the real Saswin was safe with his daughter in Seattle didn't change how I felt.

But those mannequins.

The blobs they'd become.

I shuddered just thinking about it. As I taped up the box of Jake's books, I imagined the walls of Marissa's bedroom retreating from me, leaving me in a desert of carpet.

I wouldn't suffer the same fate as Jimmy. I had a family to look after.

Still, the Saswin-thing was alone and it made my stomach twist. It didn't matter if it was my old friend or if it was a minor deity who only understood people inasmuch as he interacted with them—he was confused and scared at being left behind, and I could vividly feel his helpless mental riot.

The question I'd been struggling to sculpt out of my worries finally showed itself:

Why didn't the god leave?

He wanted to be around people, there weren't people anymore at Cloverleaf Mall, so why didn't he go somewhere else? There was an outdoor mall north of the river that was still popular. Or several shopping hotspots through the city and suburbs.

Why didn't he go there?

If he did, then the hustle and bustle of retail culture should overcome his loneliness or weakness or whatever the dying mall was doing to him.

The similarity to my own predicament wasn't lost on me.

I didn't want to leave my home, either.

I wanted Marissa to start this great new career, even if it meant moving away. I wanted her to have her own place and be able to care for herself and redevelop all the confidence that her failed relationship had stolen.

At the same time, I liked her under my roof because then I knew she was safe. I could still guide her toward the same success and happiness that Hank and I had built.

But underneath my desires for my daughter were my desires for myself.

I was *this* person, who lived in south Richmond and helped keep Dillard's and the Cloverleaf Mall alive. And in my family—in my house—I was *Mom*.

When Marissa moved, I'd be part of her extended family. I'd be *Grandma*. As thrilled as Jake might be to visit Grandma and Grandpa, the fact that it'd be 'visiting' would cement us as *outside* the family.

But if Hank and I moved with them, I'd no longer be Lisa who kept Dillard's afloat and in the evenings settled into the cozy home I'd built with my husband.

And here's the real kicker that I hated admitting to myself—if I followed my daughter across the state, then which of us was the matriarch? Which of us was *Mom*?

That was a selfish thought and I was immediately ashamed of it.

But from the mixed up soup of thought comparing myself to the Saswin-thing, that's what popped out.

A self-aware revelation that didn't help me one bit.

It didn't make the decision about moving any easier.

And right then, as I carried a box of books to the garage, it didn't change my gut-twisting worry for the Saswin-thing.

In fact, it was so much nicer to imagine ways of helping Saswin than to face the spiraling chaos inside my head. My problem had no perfect solution. But for the Saswin-thing, if I could convince him to move, then he'd be happy again.

He was lonely and scared and confused why everyone had left. He needed to go somewhere else where there were people.

I could take him to that mall north of the river. Or to Carytown in the city—lots of shopping foot traffic there. Or the university downtown. If he needed to be around people, that was the place to be.

Hank called for me, and in his tone I could hear him wanting to discuss our plans once again.

But Saswin needed me. He shouldn't spend one more night in that empty mall.

Packing for Marissa could wait until tomorrow.

I would go back to Cloverleaf and offer to take Saswin somewhere else.

21

———

THIS WAS A BAD IDEA, but if I allowed space in my mind to consider that, then I also needed to consider Marissa's invitation, so I instead plowed forward with my plan: take the Saswin-thing somewhere with more people.

I put my shoes back on, grabbed my coat, and then walked through the living room to the garage.

Before I could get in the car, Marissa stumbled into the garage behind me, hopping into her shoes. "Where are you headed? Let me tag along."

No, this was exactly what I was trying to get away from. "I have something to take care of at work."

Marissa checked the time on her phone. "At nine-thirty? Can we talk?"

"Tomorrow's better."

"You keep saying that." Her intonation drifted toward, *I'm putting my foot down.* But she caught herself, and instead asked for help. "I just want your advice on something, Mom."

She was handling me. Approaching the topic in a way she knew would be disarming. This was the first time I'd noticed, but probably not the first time it'd happened. How long had she been doing this? How many times had she talked in a circle to avoid Mom getting mad?

"Of course. Whatever you need." I said it sincerely. Even if Marissa was trying to manipulate me, I could still maintain my role of mother by helping her. Call her bluff and show her that I was still her mom.

"Maybe we drive around a bit," Marissa said.

I sighed. "Sure."

I wanted to get to the mall and help Saswin, not have this conversation. But there'd be no getting Marissa out of the car until she'd said her fill. My only option was to let her talk, drop her off back home, and then head back out.

I asked, "Does your father know he's responsible if Jake wakes up?"

"I told him."

I backed out of the garage into the night.

"Did you find your friend?" Marissa asked.

"No, but his daughter responded to me on Facebook. He's with her." I left out the part about them being 3,000 miles away.

Marissa breathed deeply, always a sign she was working herself up to say something difficult. "Mom, I could use your help in Fairfax. Dad's help, too."

I wasn't falling for the *you're-still-useful* routine. "I

appreciate you trying to make us feel needed, but you've already told us your salary. You can afford daycare just fine. And we'll be up on our days off."

"I'm not talking logistics. I mean—yes, it'll be super helpful to have you there—but what I'm saying is that we've been living with you for a year now. Jake spends as much time with you as he does with me. You're part of his life. I hate to lose that. I'm already taking him away from the only home he knows. I don't want him to suddenly only see Grandpa and Grandma once a week."

That was a bitter cup to swallow. I didn't want my grandson to be confused about why I wasn't around much anymore. "Maybe we could come up an extra evening or two each week."

"I'd still miss you."

That felt too close to a paradigm shift between mother and daughter. I tried to squash down my irritation but failed. "You're the one leaving."

"I found a job!" She took a deep breath, showing more self-control than I was, which also irritated me. "Mom, I like living with you. I like that us chatting is a regular part of my day and that I can ask you for advice whenever."

She was trying to make peace but I'd been frustrated about this for months and it was all coming out. "You didn't take my advice about this job."

"Of course not. This job is a whole different level than what I've had before. And name one other time in my adulthood that I haven't taken your advice."

I readied a list to spit back at her but discovered it was empty.

"Mom, this is my step up. I'd like to move back to Richmond one day, but I need this first job. After a couple years of experience, a whole career opens up."

"So this move might be temporary?" That could change things. This was too much think through right now.

"There's no guarantees, but I'd like it to be. I don't want to be away from you and Dad. I need you guys."

We were at a stoplight so I studied my daughter's face. Was she only telling me what I wanted to hear? I decided I believed her. So why was I still so angry about her moving? I needed to be needed, but now she said she needed me, and I still felt so agitated.

I drove to the next stoplight in silence.

Mom's weren't supposed to get so mad at their kids.

And there it was.

Mom.

I was *Mom.*

Marissa needed me, but being needed didn't change the fact that me moving to Fairfax would leave behind who I was. And it would speed up this shifting of our relationship.

"I just don't want things to change," I said.

My daughter reached over to hold my hand.

When had her hands turned into those of an adult?

Marissa was the baby who'd been in breach until I'd pushed with just the right muscles, which I was able to do because I refused the epidural. Marissa was the toddler who held on to my index finger while she learned to walk. She was the kindergartner who asked me to say the word trolley 20 times in a row until she could make all the consonant sounds herself. She was the high schooler who asked me how to deal with a boy who wouldn't leave her alone. She was the college student who asked me what kitchenware to buy and what sort of bedsheets I liked best. She was the young wife who wanted to know if I thought it counted as abuse when it was just words.

She was my friend, who I sometimes asked for advice. I liked where we were.

If *I* moved in with *her*, all that flipped on its head.

"Where are we going?" Marissa asked.

"Just driving." My thoughts were now miles away from my earlier intention to help the Saswin-thing.

Except, apparently they weren't.

"We're at the mall." Marissa pointed to the big stucco building with the Dillard's sign out front, the low mall sprawling out behind it.

How had I done that? I'd been so lost in our conversation that I'd driven my normal route to work. Or had something been influencing my subconscious decisions?

I pulled into the lot and parked right out front.

"I get that it's a big reversal," Marissa said, "you following me around."

"That's not it," I lied, surprised at how on-the-nose she was.

"Then what is it, Mom?"

A foreign thought burst into my mind with such force

that I could practically feel the direction it had come from. The Saswin-thing cried, loud enough for me to hear it outside. I hunched over, the volume hurting my ears from within.

"Mom?" Marissa's voice punched through the chaos. "Are you okay?"

The mental scream faded.

I looked up at my daughter.

In her concern, I hadn't felt *less than*. Instead, it felt like Hank's concern for me.

That was a nice thought. Something further to consider in my big decision.

But right then, the cry for help still echoed between my ears.

"Only a headache," I reassured Marissa. "But I remembered something I have to do inside. I'll be right back."

I got out of the car, turning it off to take my keys with me.

Of course Marissa didn't stay. She followed me across the dark parking lot. "Mom, what are you talking about?"

I jabbed my keys into the door to Dillard's.

"Mom, this is weird. Why do you need to get into work right now?"

"Marissa, please stay in the car." I was stuck between protecting my daughter from what waited inside and getting to the Saswin-thing in time. I couldn't leave him alone. I couldn't let anyone feel like that.

The lock clicked open and I hurried through the

vestibule. I tried to pull the door shut behind me to lock Marissa out, but I'm not quicker than a 26-year-old.

Another mental scream for help.

I ran as quick as my joints would let me. My legs and back were so tired from the events of the day, but I had enough left in me for what I needed to do.

Marissa followed me through Dillard's. "What are you doing?"

There wasn't time to convince her not to follow me. "If you're coming with me, then you have to do what I say."

"What are you talking about, Mom?"

"Someone needs my help. And it might be dangerous."

"You're worrying me. If someone needs help, we should call the police." She doubted me enough to question me, but trusted me enough to follow. I led my daughter through Dillard's into the main drag of Cloverleaf Mall.

22

THE MALL's interior lights stayed on at night.

The skylights were black, though, which left the empty mall to be lit solely by a hospital fluorescence, and created dark, vacuous rectangles in the ceiling.

"Where are we going?" Marissa asked. "Did someone call you? Who are we helping?"

I worried about her safety, but if she stayed close to me, I could keep her from getting grabbed by the mannequins while I rescued the Saswin-thing.

We turned the corner toward the JCPenny. The Sears wing came into view.

The lights were off here.

Only a trickle of light from the main hallway made its way around the corner. As our eyes adjusted, I kept Marissa close in case I suddenly needed to pull her away from a blob of plastic limbs.

"I thought they kept it all lit at night," Marissa said.

I turned on my phone's flashlight. It showed us ten feet ahead and then vague outlines past that. I didn't see any mannequins or conglomerations. I took my daughter's hand. "This way."

"Did your friend call you? Is he not really with his daughter?"

I didn't know how to answer, but Marissa was still following, so I kept moving.

I felt another surge of the god's emotion, a blending of fear and a plea for help. "Hurry," I said to Marissa.

In the dark, the Sears wing felt too much like the expanse I'd been stuck in yesterday.

I pulled my daughter quickly around the dry decorative fountain, past the closed knife shop where I'd found my way back to Hank, and again to the papered-over glass doors of the Sears.

I pulled open the unlocked door.

The darkness inside the Sears felt heavy.

"Okay, now this is trespassing," Marissa said, but she'd inherited my need to help people, and if I said someone was in need, she was on board. She didn't think me so old and feeble that I'd be imagining the whole thing, although as I walked confidently into the unnervingly dark store, she had to have her doubts.

Marissa turned on the flashlight on her own phone, which reached farther than mine. Light spilled over the eight escalators, seven of them still ascending.

"What the hell?" Marissa said. She'd barely been a teenager when Sears had shut its doors, but you didn't need vivid memories of 90s shopping experiences to know that eight escalators shoulder to shoulder wasn't a normal architectural decision. "The lights are all out over here. Why is there power to the escalators?"

Again, I didn't know the answer, but I did know that the Saswin-thing was desperate for my help.

I kept my grip on Marissa's hand, as much for my own reassurance as anything. As we got closer to the lost hallway, my trepidation was waking up. It was nice to have my daughter with me.

"He's upstairs." I led us to the stopped escalator.

"No," Marissa said. "Broken escalators are dangerous."

It wasn't worth protesting, so we rode up to the second floor. The metal steps hummed under my feet.

The darkness grew in weight, so much that now Marissa felt it. "This is too much. You have to tell me what's going on. If your friend's asking you to come up here, he probably has bad intentions. We should leave."

I had to admit, Marissa had a better sense for danger than I did. Call it a result of her last relationship.

But she didn't know the full situation. This wasn't Saswin luring me up here to steal my purse. There was something—someone—in need.

She was right about the danger, though. She had to be ready. "It's going to get weird," I told her. "You need to do exactly what I say."

Marissa mumbled something under her breath. She tugged me back toward the escalator. "Come on," she said with patronizing exasperation. "I shouldn't have let you come in here at all."

Damn, the nerve of her. "I'm helping someone," I responded sharply. "You can come along or go back to the car."

Marissa held tight to my hand, considering whether to force me back outside.

I jerked away to show her I still had plenty of strength.

She followed along.

I found the side hallway easily enough, and as we approached the corner, I warned Marissa, "Here's where it gets strange."

We came around the corner and the god's lost hallway was suddenly before us, as claustrophobic and brightly lit as ever.

I could swear the ceiling was another foot lower; now I could nearly reach up and touch it.

The shops were still packed floor-to-ceiling with merchandise that pressed up against invisible barriers at their fronts. Slot canyons disappeared inside.

There was one thing that felt less claustrophobic, though: The clutter in the middle of the hallway—the benches and kiosks all squeezed in together were gone. It was a straight shot to where we'd found the lonely god earlier this evening.

Where the shops' invisible barriers had given out, and merchandise had flooded out into the hallway, now there were two wide, round trenches carved in the layers of books, clothes, toys, and calendars.

The blobs of mannequin plastic had progressed down the hallway, gathering up material as they went.

Where the Saswin-thing had stood before, the mall detritus gathered along the walls all the way up to the ceiling, where it formed an arch over the top. Altogether, it transformed the lost hallway into a tunnel made from the mall's offerings.

Except now something blocked that tunnel.

The two carved paths in the layers of merchandise met at the mouth of the tunnel. Deep within, at least the distance of the hallway itself, a rounded wall of shiny white plastic clogged the strange artery. Limbs stuck out from it, along with gathered clothes, books, and toys. I saw the edges of a bench and kiosk poking out.

I didn't see Saswin.

My stomach dropped.

Is this why the mannequins were gathering together—why I'd had the sense they were building towards something? To turn on their creator and force the world away from him?

I had to get to Saswin. If they'd already yanked him away, then I'd touch their plastic flesh to go get him back. He didn't think that'd work, but I had to try something.

I started down the hallway. Marissa grabbed me and this time she didn't let go.

"What is this place?" she hissed.

I tried to yank free but lacked the strength. "He needs my help."

"Is this like a movie set? It's something out of a nightmare."

"So help me get him out of here."

"Who?"

Her familiar stubbornness was infuriating. "Saswin but not Saswin. I don't have time to explain it. Those mannequins are dragging the world away from him. We have to help *now*."

Marissa's fear of her surroundings turned into fear for me. There were no mannequins in the hallway she could see. She was watching her mom lose her mind.

"I'm not senile yet." I took advantage of her shock to twist free.

I rushed down the hallway as fast as my aching legs would take me. The longer it took me to get to him, the farther away the Saswin-thing would be.

"Mom, please. This place feels strange. It's no wonder you're getting confused. Please, let's go."

I reached the layers of merchandise and had to slow down. The hallway felt even tighter with the piles of *stuff* atop the floor and up the walls.

Marissa could have locked her arms around me but chose not to. "I can't be in here. It feels like a closet."

How had I forgotten? Marissa had always hated tight spaces. She slept terribly as a baby until we tossed the crib and got her a real bed. At daycare, she'd once wound up stuck in a closet. The teachers had to call me out of work to come calm her down.

This lost hallway was the epitome of a confining space,

especially here where the stores spewed out their wares into an even more restricting tunnel.

I should have thought of that as soon as I realized Marissa was coming with me inside. Protecting my daughter should have been my first priority.

But my need to rescue the Saswin-thing was still there. I needed to be both the parent who shielded my daughter from fears and the person who helped those in need—especially those like me.

"I'm so sorry, but we can't leave yet."

"I can't stay here with you," Marissa said. "I want to help you through whatever's going on in your head and with...this." She gestured to the tunnel ahead, still unaware that what looked like the tunnel's end was actually a mass of vindictive plastic mannequins. "But it's all too much."

The Saswin-thing reached out with his transfer of emotion once again, a cry for help, this time drenched in a deadly urgency.

"I'm coming," I said with the same tone I used for Jake when I wanted to reassure him that everything was okay, even when I didn't know for sure.

I moved as quick as I dared over the layers of merchandise. "How do I help you?" I called.

"Mom!" Marissa shrieked with such fear that I turned back around.

Behind her, in the empty stretch of the lost hallway, bits of mannequin now dotted the floor. Hands covered in dozens of fingers, heads pulled along by arms, knees inch-worming along, all frozen in place by my gaze.

A trio of forearms joined at the elbow was stuck in the act of pinwheeling out from a clothing store, emerging from the slot canyon that disappeared into the mountains of clothing.

The mannequin conglomeration hadn't absorbed everything. It had left some bits behind to trap us.

"Keep your eyes on them," I ordered my daughter. "They can't move if you're looking at them."

Panic in her widening eyes. "What?"

In a few moments, she'd either flee or collapse on the floor in a panic attack. Either way would leave her vulnerable to the mannequin pieces touching her and pushing me away from her forever.

While we'd locked eyes, the crawling limbs advanced.

Marissa looked again. "How did they get closer?" she wailed.

"Don't let them touch you!"

All my warning did was agitate Marissa's panic. She made a lurching start in an attempt to flee, but the scattered mannequin pieces were too much for her and she froze.

I saw my scared daughter and nothing else mattered. I headed back. "It's okay. I'll get you out of here. It's okay."

"Mom, I can't do this. Whatever we're doing, I can't do it. I have to leave. Please come with me."

"Yes, you can leave, I promise." I needed a way to get her to safety without abandoning Saswin. "Run for the exit. I'll watch the mannequin bits so they can't move. Once you get back to Sears, run straight for the car."

"Not without you," she sobbed.

"I'll be right behind you. I have to do one thing to help first."

"I'm not leaving you."

"Go!" I ordered with a faked mania. If Marissa thought I was off my rocker, maybe she'd decide I couldn't be saved.

It worked.

My daughter looked at me like I was a stranger and then she ran.

I stared hard at the failed mannequin creations as Marissa disappeared into the dark Sears. I watched long enough that I was sure she'd made it back down the escalators.

Then I turned back to the distant mass of mannequin plastic that had taken my friend.

I headed into the tunnel. Menswear stuck to the ceiling, drooping in places. Humidity hung in the air. Muffled music came from deeper within the tunnel, past the plastic blockage. I thought they might be children's Christmas songs, like played in toy stores starting after Halloween.

I climbed over merchandise, frequently glancing backwards to keep the mannequin bits from getting close.

As I approached the blob, I noticed that its surface didn't look so smooth and shiny anymore. It had absorbed too much. Books and lotion bottles and knives and a thousand other reminders of the mall's heyday poked out. A black sock dangled from the palm of an outreached plastic hand.

I swallowed my fear.

The Saswin-thing needed my help, and I was someone who took care of others.

I marched to the mannequin amalgamation like I was about to dole out punishment to a young child. But instead of delivering a blazing lecture, I reached out to touch the smooth plastic with a single finger.

Far behind me, Marissa screamed. "Mom!"

She hadn't left me.

In her cry I heard my grandson calling for one of us after a nightmare. I'd heard Marissa the same way when she was five, calling for me and Hank.

Clarity fell over me. What was I doing? I couldn't risk the mannequins dragging the world away from me in order to chase after the Saswin-thing. My heart bled for him, but I didn't know what he was. I didn't know if getting dragged away by the mannequins was as deadly for him as it would be for me. I was about to risk my life with my husband and daughter and grandson in order to...what?

I took a careful backwards step toward Marissa.

The lonely god chose that moment to reach out again. Its cry for help pierced my mind and vibrated my nerves from the tips of my toes up to behind my eyes.

I blinked.

More slowly than I meant to.

A hand reached out from the plastic blob to close

around my ankle and push away this lost corner of a dying mall.

23

____

DROOPING shirts above me rocketed upward.

Stacks of board games and DVDS shot away to my right, while a pile of lingerie withdrew to my left.

Even as I sensed the tunnel widening, I heard Marissa's terrified scream at my disappearance, followed by her shoes slapping the tile floor as she ran—in which direction I couldn't say.

I kicked the mannequin hand off my ankle, and then backed away.

My heart raced.

The layered tunnel floor now stretched a hundred feet to either side. The walk back out into the lost hallway was at least three times that.

I should have never got so close, let alone my stupid plan to touch the damn thing on purpose. I needed to walk back, to escape back to my family.

But I was here. Maybe I could help.

"Saswin?" I called.

His emotions flooded into me.

They felt different from before. Quieter. More distant.

He was begging for help.

"What can I do?" I yelled into the cavernous space. "I came back to take you somewhere else. There's other places where more people visit. Where are you?"

It answered with an image that I couldn't understand. It felt gray, but not like the color as much as the visual effect the world gets when you're about to pass out.

"Can you come to me? I can carry you somewhere better."

It's hard to explain what happened next. I think he tried to latch onto me. Although I saw nothing but the wide tunnel, I felt arms reach around my shoulders and neck. Fingers dug into my shoulder blades as they tried to hang on. I remembered Marissa clinging to me that way as a toddler when she was scared. Jake now did the same. He would nuzzle into us when he needed a good "I'm recovered but that was scary" sort of cry.

Despite feeling the Saswin-thing's grip on me, I had the sense that his physical form and real self was miles away. He was clinging to me via a long mental thread.

Regardless, I would carry him like I'd carried my daughter and grandson.

"Are you hanging on?" I asked.

I received an affirmative cloud of emotion.

There was nothing to do now but walk to the exit.

Keeping my eyes on the fallen mannequin, I took a few exploratory steps.

The Saswin-thing's weight was substantial, even though he wasn't physically with me. My shoulders and thighs ached. I wasn't sure my lower back could take it.

I checked quickly over my shoulder. The bits of mannequin had been left behind by the expanding space. They weren't a threat until I escaped.

When I turned back around, however, the blob had advanced to nearly an arm's reach.

My heart leapt but I stayed on my feet.

With my eyes glued to the monstrous lump of plastic and my body weighed down by a lonely god clinging onto me from so far away, I walked carefully backwards.

A minute. Five. Ten.

My shoulders hurt. My back compressed.

"Where are you?" I asked.

Two gentle tugs.

He was still back there somewhere. I was still dragging him to freedom.

I walked another ten minutes before I heard scraping and skittering.

I glanced behind me. The pinwheel mannequin legs froze in place atop a pile of black video game consoles. The hand covered in fingers had been scrambling over a low hill of felt jewelry boxes.

My stomach rolled with fear. I'd thought I was safe from them until I escaped my private desert. But whatever kept regular people from walking into these expanded spaces—it didn't apply to the mannequins themselves.

A lower scraping noise came from deeper inside the tunnel. The blob was on the move.

I turned sideways to keep everything in view.

"Is this working?" I asked aloud. "Otherwise, I'm risking a lot for nothing."

The Saswin-thing's weight still hung around my shoulders, but this time I didn't feel a response.

I managed to get on the far side of the hand and legs and keep moving.

Before long, I heard irregular footsteps. I looked as quick as I could to find two connected legs frozen in an inchworm's arch.

Again, I maneuvered around it to keep all my pursuers in view.

When it happened a third time, it got trickier not to lose sight of one of them.

More behind me now, in my path.

Too many.

I turned to pin them in place, only to hear those behind me start shuffling.

"If you can do something to help," I said loudly, "now's the time."

The Saswin-thing squeezed me more tightly. I instinctively reached up to pat it on the back, but felt nothing material.

The farther I walked, the more tension I felt from the

Saswin-thing's grip, as if the tendrils that held us together were stretching thin.

It did the same to my nerves.

I needed to get him out. I couldn't leave him here alone while the world left him behind.

I walked on, pulling the invisible connection tighter, and increasing the tension with which it pulled back at me.

"You have to help me out," I said. "Walk with me."

Finally, some coherent conversation came through, emotion that I could actually translate into words:

Come back.

He tugged on our mental threads.

Stay here and bring others.

I'd understood this all wrong.

He wasn't holding on so I could pull him free. He was trying to keep me there.

"No." I spoke as I did to Marissa when she'd disobeyed me as a child. "You need people around, right? There's other places. I'll take you there."

He raised his voice, so to speak.

I live HERE.

The connection between us thickened, allowing me to sense the distance between us:

Farther than I'd walked as I tried to drag him free. Farther than I'd walked in my entire life.

The mental connection stretched from me, down a massive cavern made from Cloverleaf's shopping trea-sures, through a den that the lonely god must have called home. Then past that, the tendrils connecting us stretched ever deeper into the lonely god's private hell where everyone and everything else had been pushed away, were still being pushed away. The plastic people the Saswin-thing had created held him tight as they raced ever more distant, fulfilling their accidental purpose until there were miles between us, entire lengths of interstates, the farthest any manmade creation had ever traveled through the stars, the farthest I could imagine the edge of the universe extending. Except the mental thread forced me to imagine it, every step over shopping mall tile floor, the desert inter-rupted by sparse decorative fountains and cell-phone dealer kiosks, the edges of my pilgrimage watched by distant clothing shops and bookstores and other dying markets. In less than a moment, it inserted into my head the memory of that still-continuing journey.

Loneliness struck me like a falling pallet.

The shock of it made me shudder in some internal way.

Saswin lost his grip.

He was there clinging onto me and then he was gone.

His loss reverberated through my mind to leave me dazed.

Marissa's voice appeared behind me, midway through a shout as if her volume had suddenly been cranked up.

"Where are you?" she shouted.

The memory of my journey—the god's journey?—took up so much space that it was difficult to focus on why my daughter was yelling for me.

Every time I looked away from the mannequin blob and the little pieces around it, they moved closer.

I kept my eyes on the mannequins and followed the sound of my daughter's voice, heading past the distant storefronts in this lost hallway of Cloverleaf Mall.

I wanted to help the Saswin-thing, but I was unfathomably far away from him now.

"Mom!"

Marissa shouted again as the lost hallway snapped back into place.

My daughter had journeyed into the claustrophobic tunnel to retrieve me. She saw me at the end of my jaunt, popping back into reality.

She wrapped me in a tight hug. "Can we go, please?"

Her warmth pulled me out of my daze. "Yes," I assured her. "I'll get you out of here."

I kept my eyes on the mannequin blob, still deep within the tunnel. Marissa watched the hands and feet and legs as we maneuvered past them, all the way back to Sears.

Before we crossed into the dark, I felt a final cry of anguish. It came from nauseatingly far away. There was nothing I could do.

Back in the upper floor of Sears, I turned around to see the lost hallway had vanished, or at least the entrance had. Either way, it took the mannequins and the lonely god with it.

We found our way to the escalators—only two of them now—and back to the Sears wing.

I walked beside my daughter to the car, trying to understand what had happened.

I'd gone in to save the Saswin-thing. To this day, I'm still not sure if that was because he was manipulating me somehow, or because my heart really was breaking for him.

I started the car but sat there.

Marissa and I hadn't spoken a word since we'd left the lost hallway.

Finally, she spoke, only to explain her return. "I called Dad. He yelled at me to go back for you."

I didn't know what to say. "Thank you," seemed to fit. I drove us home.

EPILOGUE

When we listed our house, it jumped straight into a bidding war. That left us with plenty of money to enjoy life with Marissa and Jake in Fairfax.

Not enough to let Hank stay on the name brand medicine, but so far the generic has been working. Fingers crossed.

Jake is growing so fast. Whenever he wants us, he knows we're just one bedroom over, and I think that's great.

He's saying a few words now. *"Ous"* for "outside" and *"ot"* for "blocks."

Marissa calls us "Grandma" and "Grandpa," so Jake doesn't get confused.

Marissa feels guilty, because she assumes that when I get home from my assistant manager job at TJ Maxx and I'm staring off into space, or when we're at the dinner table and Hank has to ask me three times to pass the peas, or when I'm playing *Frozen* with Jake and I mix up which sister has ice powers, it must mean moving was a minor trauma that's accelerated my mental decline.

But it's not that my thoughts get foggy. They're crystal clear, even when I wish they weren't.

It's not that my mind wanders. Or at least, "wander" is the wrong word. It would imply a randomness to where my thoughts go.

But the moment I stop actively focusing on something, my mind heads straight to the same fearful spot every time:

I'm back with Saswin, riding that force of the mannequins pushing away the world, keeping pace with the expansion of the universe.

WHY I WROTE THIS BOOK

Let's talk about endings.

If you've read a few of my books, you might have noticed that I love when the climax of the plot syncs up with an emotional epiphany of the main character.

Think of *The Empire Strikes Back*: Luke spends the movie denying that he could ever slip to the dark side. "Good" doesn't lose. That's how simple he sees it. He'll face the villain and save his friends. But then in the climactic duel, Darth Vader reveals that he's Luke's father, and Luke has this epiphany that good can lose. His good father turned evil. With this realization, Luke stops trying to defeat Darth Vader before he's ready and instead escapes to regroup and actually start listening to Yoda.

I do something similar in *I Found Christmas Lights Slithering Up My Street*, *Those Who Dwell Below the Sidewalk*, and each book of my trilogy *Horror Lurks Beneath*.

It's a solid template.

I view writing a book not as creating a product to sell or as piece of art to be admired, but rather an emotional experience I'm creating for you, Strange Reader.

And an epiphany that allows you to conquer evil, right when all seems lost? That sets off all sorts of happy brain chemicals. You gotta love it.

So in the first draft of *I Found a Lost Hallway in a Dying Mall*, the climax was very different from what you just read.

In the chaos of realizing that the lonely god was trying to keep her there, Lisa played a more active role in freeing herself from its grip. She had a realization about who she was and her relationship with her daughter, and that gave her the mental awareness to break free from the mall and decide to move with Marissa.

If I'd polished it up, maybe it'd have been a narratively satisfying ending.

Or maybe you're already noticing the problem there.

Luke Skywalker's epiphany was simple: evil is a real threat and a real temptation, and thus requires real effort to defeat.

If you haven't read *I Found Christmas Lights Slithering Up My Street*, I'll give you a minor spoiler. The main character's climactic epiphany is also simple: grief shouldn't erase his existence.

But for my friend Lisa there could be no simple epiphany.

Her situation doesn't have a "right" answer.

I'm confident in that, because I've been writing about Lisa for ten years.

She's not real.

At least, she's not a single person whom I personally know.

In my day job, I work in marketing. For the past ten years, I've had a full-time retainer with a health company that produces books, online classes, and other products. I write sales copy. Emails, landing pages, video scripts—you name it. If something needs to be written and its intention is to persuade, it's my job to write it.

To do that, you create an "avatar." Not a blue-skinned *FernGully* knockoff, and not a bald kid with superpowers, but a representation of our ideal customer.

We mostly sell to Baby-Boomers, so I invented a character who I pretended to talk to when I wrote my marketing copy.

She needed a name, so I googled "What were the most popular baby names in the 1950s?"

For a boy, it was James. For a girl, it was Lisa.

(Okay, it was Linda, but at some point I got my wires crossed and ended up sticking with Lisa.)

I wrote up this big spreadsheet about Lisa's biggest desires, her biggest worries, her biggest pet peeves. If you squished all our most likely customers together like a big mannequin blob, the woman you'd get is Lisa.

Toward the start of my career, I wrote to a Lisa who didn't want to grow old. She didn't want her arthritis to get worse. She didn't want to need stronger prescription glasses.

I did okay. Well enough to not get fired.

Then I realized something obvious. It was true about me, why wouldn't it be true about 63-year-old, pretend Lisa?

More than our own physical ailments, we care about our relationships.

We care what our children think about us.

My kids are still little, but when my 5-year-old says, "Daddy, put your phone down and watch *X-men* with me," there's a fist-sized ball of guilt that makes me worry they'll remember me as always on my phone.

I can only imagine that as my little boy and two little girls turn into adults, I'm going to want them to still see me as smart, as superman, as someone with fun ideas, as someone they can trust. Like the Lisa in this book, I'm sure I'll want them to rely on me, even as I contradictorily want them to become self-reliant.

When these ideas occurred to me—or I read them somewhere, who can remember—and I was thinking through how to apply them to my marketing work, I happened to have a building inspector over for some concerns with my house. Guy in his late 50s. And the man told me three or four times ways that he helped his adult son with his own home projects—stuff his son didn't know how to do and thus still relied on his dad for. He got so happy and excited every time there was a chance to relay one of those stories.

I must have looked like a space cadet zoning out, because my mind immediately dashed off to this epiphany —holy shit, this guy is the living embodiment of this core desire—to continue to take care of our kids. Or maybe to continue to be needed by them. Something like that.

There's probably varying levels of healthiness and toxicity to this desire.

But you see what I mean about it not being simple.

Sure, I could make simple promises in my marketing materials. A book from a doctor about healthy habits for blood sugar could keep your blood sugar levels balanced, which in turn will have your kids worrying about you less. A video course of Tai Chi for joint pain could keep your joints exercised and thus less swollen, so you can get about easier and your kids won't see you limping and think they need to take care of you.

But I've been mentally living in this problem several hours a day for ten years. These little promises are great (and I'm proud of the ways these products have helped people—it's really cool to hear their stories afterwards), but they only help little pieces of the real issue.

Your kid may be happy that you're not chugging full-sugar Pepsi with every meal, and they may be excited that you can chase the grandkids around the yard without pain, but does that really cure your self-doubt that your kids are now quicker thinkers than you? That they've got 30 years of career potential ahead of them, while you've just retired, signaling that you're done improving the primary skill that kept your family fed? That as their lives get busier, your wellbeing is becoming an item on their checklist, when only a few years ago their wellbeing was your whole world?

It's complicated.

You'll notice that the emotional core of the first three *I Found Horror* books are experiences or worries that I've been through myself as an Elder Millennial. Early fatherhood, grief, nostalgia.

This book started with the setting. I wanted to write about a creepy mall. I'd read Volume 1 of Adam Cesare's graphic novel *Dead Mall*, and I'd watched YouTube creator Kane Pixel's series *The Oldest View*. I highly recommend both. I loved the experience of those stories and I wanted to keep living inside them, so I decided to write my own.

I needed a character and story. And I wanted to branch out—not just write about myself again. But I also wanted it to be about a near-universal emotional struggle.

And so naturally, my mind went to Lisa. The avatar who I spend so much time with each workday.

I slowly crafted this moment in Lisa's life when she's most worried about this core issue of identity in relation to her daughter. I gave her a decision to make that represented this internal conflict: her daughter inviting her to move in.

And then I set Lisa loose in this creepy mall.

Like I said, in the first draft I tried to write her a nice ending: epiphany about the self leads to success against the antagonist.

But Lisa's problem isn't simple.

That's why I was able to make a marketing career out of helping just little bits of it.

And so if I tried to write Lisa making the "right" decision, it felt wrong.

I wasn't going to declare the proper decision for Lisa to make. I'm a thirty-seven-year-old writer. I don't know what she should do.

So in the next drafts, I set my goal to leave you, Strange Reader, with an unsettled feeling. Lisa and Hank have moved in with Marissa and Jake. We don't get to see Lisa's exact reasoning for agreeing to it. I tried to hint in the end that maybe it was out of fear of becoming like the lonely god. But I also tried to avoid declaring that as a fact.

We know that Lisa will now get to be a unique person in her grandson's life—not just extended family who visits sometimes. We know that they're taking a risk with losing health insurance and Hank going off the brand name meds.

We know that all the good and bad that Lisa expected from this decision is coming to fruition.

This is the decision she made, but I tried very hard to avoid declaring whether it was the right decision, let alone whether it was made for the right reasons.

Narratively, it's not the sort of ending I usually aim for. It might not *feel* like an ending as much as some of my other books.

In fact, this book missed my original release goal by several months, because after I wrote this final ending, I questioned it and reworked it and talked with my writer friends about how it could be both narratively satisfying and not oversimplify Lisa's emotional struggle.

Finally, after letting it sit for a few weeks, I came back and read it again. Yes, it's messy. No, there's not a hugely satisfying moment in the climax where all the pieces come together to deliver the perfect epiphany. But the moment I decided to write about Lisa's struggles with identity and her daughter, I gave up any chance of a cut-and-dry ending where epiphany equals victory.

I like to look at my books not as a product to be sold or a work of art to be admired, but an emotional experience I'm creating for you. This one is like a lot of life's problems: there's no single epiphany that can solve everything. Instead, all we can do is hang on tight and—alongside our friend Lisa—ride the expansion of the universe.

-Ben Farthing, June 2024

READ THIS NEXT

Hello Strange Reader,

Stephen King has Constant Readers. But you just read a book about mutating mannequins dragging a lonely god into an infinite journey. I figure you'll proudly wear the mantle of "Strange Reader."

And so, Strange Reader, *thank you* for reading.

Please take a few seconds to rate it or even write out a review. I read them all, and I appreciate the good and the bad. They help my weird little books find more homes.

If you want to stay up to date with my new releases, plus hear my book recommendations for Strange Readers like you and me, you can sign up for my email newsletter at BenFarthing.com.

If you'd like to order a signed copy of this or other books, or grab stickers, fridge magnets, or other merch, go to my etsy store: TheDreadFarthing.

You've now seen my style of weird horror in creepy places, with plots driven by the urge to discover *what the hell is happening?*

From here, I recommend *Those Who Dwell Below the Sidewalk.* Here's what it's about:

Beneath the city, they are watching...

During a bumper-to-bumper commute, Everard is almost murdered by a woman whose skin is covered in a living swarm of holes. Furious, Everard chases her down an impossible staircase. He's thrown into the city's supernatural underbelly where nightmares lurk around every corner.

In this world within the city's periphery, strange cults protect their members from monsters of urban legends. But something is riling up those monsters. Something ancient and evil, which has set its hungry sights on Everard.

For fans of horror epics like Stephen King's *Dark Tower* or the wondrous horrors of Clive Barker's *Cabal* & *Nightbreed*, Ben Farthing's *The Who Dwell Below the Sidewalk* is "non-stop terrifying action" with a villain who *Apex Magazine* Editor Lesley Conner called, "The stuff of my freaking nightmares."

Those Who Dwell Below the Sidewalk is available as an ebook, paperback, and audiobook.

Keep reading for a look at my other books.

IT WAITS ON THE TOP FLOOR

The tower appeared overnight, but it wants to keep you forever.

"If you like dark, twisted, raise-the-hair-on-the-back-of-your-neck horror, you can't go wrong with this book!" - Booknerdia

Thursday night, it was a dirt lot.

Friday morning, it was a 60-story skyscraper.

A tech billionaire wants the building's secrets for herself. She hires a team to reverse-engineer the overnight construction. But she knows more than she's letting on.

A curious 9-year-old decides there's treasure inside, and goes exploring. His terrified dad chases close behind. Inside, the facade of an empty office building is quickly shattered. Ghostly figures stalk the explorers. The walls themselves are hungry. And something is waiting on the top floor.

It Waits On the Top Floor is the first book in the *Horror Lurks Beneath* trilogy. It's available as an ebook, paperback, and audiobook.

THE PIPER'S GRAVEYARD

A mysterious evil haunts a small town's radio waves.

★ ★ ★ ★ ★ *"A scary atmosphere and great characters."* *Goodreads Review.*

Cessy returns home to search for her missing sister.

She finds a half-abandoned town under siege by unexplainable threats: Attics and crawlspaces stretch into endless tunnels. Corpses turn up riddled with holes— holes that slither through flesh like insectile parasites. It all leads deep into the abandoned coal mine.

Cessy's sister disappeared while investigating the vengeful voice on the radio. To find her, Cessy will have to unravel the dark mystery wriggling up from the coal mine.

The Piper's Graveyard is available as an ebook, paperback, and audiobook.

CROWDED CHASMS: TALES IN TERRIFYING PLACES

Short Stories Set in Weird and Scary Places

Lost in an endless forest, a spelling-bee champ follows the powerlines far above. But where do they lead?

In the steam tunnels under the school, a student finds a bone tied in a knot. He should have left it there.

After their minivan swerves off a cliff, a family wakes up in an empty Heaven.

Two spelunkers release an ancient evil. Their only hope is to find order in the demon's chaos.

In this collection of Weird Horror stories, Ben Farthing delivers his unique brand of surreal horror and strange happenings.

Crowded Chasms is currently available as an ebook. Paperback and audiobook are in production.

ABOUT THE AUTHOR

Ben Farthing writes supernatural horror. He lives with his wife and children near Richmond, Virginia. Follow him on Facebook, Instagram, and TikTok.